HIDDEN IDENTITY

ANGEL LAPOINT

Jumpmaster Press
Birmingham, AL

Cover Art copyright: Mariusz Patrzyk Image ID: 325299935

Library Cataloging Data

Names: Angel LaPoint, 1991 -

Title: Hidden Identity / Angel LaPoint

5.5 in. × 8.5 in. (13.97 cm × 21.59 cm)

Description: Jumpmaster Press™ digital eBook edition | Jumpmaster Press™ Trade paperback edition | Alabama: Jumpmaster Press™, 2018. P.O Box 1774 Alabaster, AL 35007 info@jumpmasterpress.com

Summary: Following disturbing visions of a mysterious woman abducting her sister, Eirian flees for safety with baby Aubree in tow. After years of keeping their secret, Aubree is discovered by agents of their old enemy and forced to confront her family's secret. Aided by companions, hiding their own enigmas, Aubree and her new friend Reima will do whatever it takes to keep her family together, while discovering mysteries they never believed possible.

ISBN-13: 978-1-949184-47-1 (eBook) | 978-1-949184-46-4 (paperback) |

1. Fantasy 2. Romance 3. Faerie 4. Mystic Realms 5. Family 6. Sisters 7. Identity

Printed in the United States of America

For more information on Angel LaPoint
Facebook.com/anivaangel2000

HIDDEN IDENTITY

ANGEL LAPOINT

*To all the broken and hurting families.
Don't give up hope.*

Acknowledgments

I want to thank my parents, Terri and Paul LaPoint, for always supporting me and encouraging me to go after my dreams. Thank you for instilling a love of reading in me from a very young age.

I want to thank my siblings, Matthew, Timothy, and Marguerite, for your words of encouragement and support.

I want to thank all my friends and family, from work, church, and everywhere else. Your enthusiasm for my stories and ideas helped keep me motivated.

I want to thank everyone at Jumpmaster Press™ for helping to make my dream a reality.

Last, but not least, I want to thank my very best friend, Emily. Your support and encouragement, all the texts and conversations, all the games we played as children, have been invaluable throughout this literary journey and into the next one and beyond.

I

Eirian opened her eyes. She sat on the dank ground of an unfamiliar, dark forest. She gagged from the damp, musty scent of the forest, strong with notes of rotting vegetation. It left a foul taste in her mouth with each breath. The black bark on the trees shone in the moonlight and curved away from the trunks in smooth, scale-like angles.

The forests surrounding her kingdom were bright, fresh, and full of life, filled with white-barked trees and colorful flowers. This forest was silent and dead.

Eirian tried to remember how she got there. She remembered dinner with her parents, the walk in the gardens with Elior, but nothing after that.

She stood and brushed the dirt and dead leaves from her dress. Her hand paused mid-motion. She did not recognize the dress. *What happened?* she wondered. *How did I get here? Did something happen?* She quickly checked herself for any injuries, and sighed in relief when she found none. That did not answer her questions about how she arrived in the desolate forest. She looked around for a path, but the strange black trees and darkness around her gave no indication of direction. Curious about the nature of the tree bark, Eirian reached out and cautiously touched the point of one of the tree scales.

"Ouch!" her voice echoed in the emptiness. She recoiled; the sharp bark cut like a razor. A bead of red appeared on the tip of her snow-white finger.

"Awww, did the princess cut herself?" a silky voice teased behind Eirian.

Eirian jumped and turned toward the voice, but saw nothing.

"You need to be careful in this forest," continued the voice. "There are many harmful things here."

"Who are you?" demanded Eirian. "Show yourself!"

A woman appeared before Eirian. Long, dark red hair trailed the ground behind her. A pale pink crystal comb held the wavy locks in place. She wore an ankle-length, forest green dress, covered in tiny gemstones that shimmered, despite the dark forest. Bracelets covered her arms, jangling with every movement. Eirian wondered how she had not noticed her before.

Eirian compared her own paper-white skin to the woman's pale pink flesh. *She speaks Elvish, but she is clearly not an Elf.*

"Who are you?" repeated Eirian.

"Who I am does not matter just yet." The woman's accent sounded strange: a strong, sultry sound with drawn out words and sharp emphasis on certain consonants. Eirian's own accent was softer; regal and refined.

"You and I have much to discuss, Princess Eirian."

"What do you mean?" asked Eirian. "What things?"

"Patience, my dear." The woman held up a hand. "All will be revealed, in time. First, we need to gain each other's trust."

"How do you expect me to trust you when you will not even tell me your name?" countered Eirian, authoritatively lifting her chin.

"There is more than one way to gain someone's trust." The woman took a slow step closer. "For example, if I were to tell you that your parents would soon come to you with exciting news, you would most likely dismiss me. At least until it came to pass."

"What news would that be?" Eirian cross her arms, irritation in her voice, and peered suspiciously at the woman.

The woman took two more steps closer and leaned in to whisper in Eirian's ear.

"Your mother is with child."

Eirian backed away, shaking her head. "You cannot know that. If my mother was with child, she would have told me."

"Ah!" The woman straightened and lifted a finger. "She does not yet know, but she will find out soon enough, and when she and your father come to you with the news, you will know I have spoken true."

Eirian opened her mouth to respond, but the mysterious woman stepped back and vanished into the trees as silently as she appeared. The space the woman left through disappeared as well. The trees pressed together, leaving Eirian no room to even slip her hand between them. She shook her head. *I'm not so foolish as to try.*

Eirian turned, looking for another route through the razor-sharp branches. The trees closed in on her with every movement. Panic filled her chest. Her heart pounded in her ears and her breath came in short bursts.

The sharp bark cut into her skin. She dropped to the ground and curled into a ball. A scream escaped her lips. "Princess! Princess! Wake up, Your Highness. You're having a nightmare!"

Eirian's eyes snapped open. She sat up in her bed and frantically checked her arms and legs for gashes. She sighed in relief; her skin remained smooth and unblemished. She rubbed her fingertip with her thumb and felt no trace of the nick from the bark. Her maid servant, Alyia, stood beside the bed, eyes wide in concern.

"Would you like me to fetch your mother?" asked Alyia.

Eirian took a deep breath and composed herself. "No, thank you, Alyia. As you said, it was only a nightmare."

"Is there anything I can do for you, Princess?"

Eirian shook her head. "I am fine. I just need a moment alone."

"Yes, Princess," Alyia bowed and backed out of the room. "I'll go make preparations for your bath."

Eirian nodded. "A bath would be good," she confessed. She felt the stench of the forest clinging to her skin. Eirian got out of bed and stood in front of her mirror. Her long, silver hair hung loose around her shoulders and nearly reached to the floor. The light grey circles under her silver eyes the only sign of her sleepless night.

"It was only a dream," she told herself, but she could not shake the ominous feeling of dread building within.

Alyia returned and Eirian turned away from her mirror. The princess bathed, slipped into her favorite powder blue gown, and went to the breakfast hall to dine with her parents.

King Alberic sat at one end of a small breakfast table made of polished white wood. Queen Livia sat to his right side. As with most elves in their region, Alberic and Livia were tall, snow-white skinned with silver hair and eyes. They both held an ageless quality, the depth of their eyes the only hint of the centuries they had lived.

Eirian silently pushed her food around her plate with her fork, occasionally taking a small bite as her limited appetite allowed.

"Eirian? Are you alright, Dear?" asked Livia. "You seem distracted."

"I am fine, Mama."

"Are you sure?" prompted Livia. "You have hardly touched your food."

Eirian looked up. "Mama, you and Daddy would not keep things from me, would you? Anything important, I mean."

"Of course not." Livia, gently laid a hand on her daughter's arm. "We keep no secrets from you. You know this."

"What is this about?" asked Alberic.

Eirian smiled in relief. "Nothing." She stood up from the table. "I should go before I am late for my lessons." Eirian kissed her mother and father on the cheek and left the dining hall.

Eirian could not shake the memory of the dream. Over the next few days, she carefully monitored her mother, watching for signs of pregnancy. She admitted to herself that she did not know the signs. The only pregnant Elf she knew – Claudette, Eirian's old nursemaid – gave birth to a baby girl, Marcia, over a year earlier. Eirian strained her ears every time she overheard her parents talking, in case they said anything about a baby. She convinced herself the entire affair – the strange woman, her mother's supposed pregnancy, the razor-bark trees – stemmed from a strange dream, a nightmare.

Eirian sat in the library with her languages tutor. She looked up when her parents entered. Her mother struggled to keep up the calm, regal demeanor she put on around others. The king and queen dismissed Eirian's tutor, and her heart raced. A pit formed in her stomach. She hid her discomfort, sat up in her chair, and patiently waited for her parents to speak. Alberic and Livia sat on one of the sofas in the room and motioned for Eirian to join them.

"Eirian," Livia took Eirian's hand in hers, "we have some news for you." Livia glanced over at her husband.

Alberic took Eirian's other hand. "You are going to be a big sister."

Livia beamed at Eirian, awaiting her response. Eirian could not move.

The voice of the woman from her dream echoed in her mind. *Your mother is with child. ...when she and your father come to you with the news, you will know I have spoken true.*

"You are with child?" asked Eirian.

14

Livia enthusiastically nodded, an expression of excitement reserved only for her family.

Eirian forced herself to smile. "That is wonderful news!" She tried to keep the tremble of fear from her voice.

Alberic patted Eirian's hand. "I am glad you are pleased."

"I knew you would be excited, just as we are." Livia gently squeezed Eirian's hand.

Eirian nodded in feigned agreement and hugged her parents. They returned her embrace and left the library. Eirian followed them to the door and watched them walk past the extravagant tapestry mural – depicting her family's legacy of establishing the kingdom – that adorned the white stone walls of the palace foyer. Their feet made no sound on the plush navy carpet as they disappeared down a side corridor. Eirian ran down the hall in the opposite direction. She ran out one of the side doors, lifting the hem of her dress so she would not trip as she raced down the cobblestone path lined with sharply manicured hedges on her way to the palace stables.

Nearing the back edge of the grounds, she called out. "Elior!"

"I'm back here," answered Elior, poking his head out of a stall near the end.

Elior was half mortal, though he still held many Elfin features. He had long, platinum hair and bright blue eyes. His ears, though shorter than a full-blooded Elf, still came to a point at the tip. His round face had soft features compared to his full-blood counterparts.

"I need to talk to you." A note of urgency tinted Eirian's voice.

A look of concern crossed Elior's face and he quickly made his way over to her.

"What's wrong?" he reached for her hand.

Eirian shook her head and pulled away. "Not here."

She turned and walked out of the stables, Elior close behind her. She led him across the grounds, to the gardens and the playhouse King Alberic commissioned for them when they were children. They outgrew the playhouse decades earlier, but still used it as a safe place to talk and spend time with one another. No one ever bothered them in their playhouse. They ducked their heads as they crawled inside and sat side-by-side, safely away from prying eyes and listening ears.

"Now, what's the matter?" Elior reached for her hand again.

This time, she let him take it. "My mother just told me she is going to have a baby."

"That's fantastic!" grinned Elior. "Why do you look so scared? Are you afraid your parents won't pay attention to you anymore?" He playfully nudged her shoulder with his own.

"No, that is not my problem." Eirian sighed and leaned her head back against the wall.

"Then what's wrong?"

Eirian took a deep breath and looked back at Elior. "You have to promise you will not tease me."

"I promise." Elior kissed the back of Eirian's hand. "Now, tell me what's bothering you."

"I had a dream," began Eirian.

"A dream?"

"More like a nightmare. I was in a forest, but the trees were unfamiliar. They were sharp and black, I cut my finger on one. All of the sudden, a woman appeared out of nowhere. She would not tell me her name, but she said we had many things to discuss."

"Did she know who you were?" asked Elior.

Eirian nodded. "I am the princess. There are few who do not know who I am. She said I would know she spoke the truth when my parents came to tell me that they were going to have a baby. The dream was two weeks ago, Elior. My parents just found out today."

"It was just a dream, Eri," Elior rubbed the back of Eirian's hand with his thumb. "I don't think you have anything to worry about."

"No, it was more than that," insisted Eirian. "Something about the woman, about her voice, the dangerous look in her eyes—I do not know how to describe the feeling she gave me, but she frightened me. I have never been this frightened."

Eirian shivered and Elior pulled her close, resting her head against his chest. He did not say anything, he simply held her and caressed her hair.

"Do you honestly believe it was just a coincidence?" asked Eirian, not leaving the comfort of Elior's embrace.

"Maybe."

"That helps," mumbled Eirian.

Elior chuckled. "Princesses shouldn't mumble."

Eirian smiled. "They also, should not secretly be in love with their servants, but I do not hear you complaining about that one." She pulled back and kissed him.

"Why would I complain about that?" asked Elior, returning the favor of another kiss. "Complaining about that would only get me in trouble."

"Thank you, Elior," sighed Eirian. "You always know how to make me feel better. I love you."

"I love you, too, Eirian."

They shared one more kiss and then left the playhouse. For the first time in a fortnight, Eirian felt unafraid.

2

Eirian went to sleep that night full of happy thoughts about her new sibling. She closed her eyes and laid her head down, expecting to feel the softness of her feather pillow and silk sheets. Instead, she opened her eyes and jumped up in horror at the damp foliage beneath her. Looking around she saw the strange, black razor-barked trees of her dream forest. The safety of her bedroom and all the comfort she found with Elior earlier in the day instantly vanished the moment she heard the sticky-sweet voice of the mysterious woman.

"See?" The woman appeared in front of Eirian wearing a long-sleeved, black velvet dress. "I told you your mother was pregnant."

"You did not tell me anything." Eirian hoped she sounded more confident than she felt. "You are not real. I am dreaming. What you told me last time was a coincidence."

"Are you sure about that?" asked the woman with a smirk. Eirian opened her mouth, but did not answer. "I was telling the truth about the baby; therefore, you should know that I am telling the truth now," continued the woman. "Yes, you are dreaming. You are correct there, but you are wrong about everything else. I am real, this forest is real, and everything I say to you here is the truth." The woman adjusted the crystal comb in her hair.

"Who are you?" asked Eirian, irritated. She did not expect the woman to answer.

"That again," scoffed the woman with a roll of her eyes. "Fine. If you insist on having a name, I will give you a name."

Eirian's eyes widened in surprise, but she quickly caught herself, returning her facial expression to an impassive mask.

"My name is Tola, though the knowledge will do you little good." Tola dismissively shook her head.

The name sounded familiar to Eirian. *Surely, I would have remembered meeting such an unpleasant and unnerving woman.*

"I still do not believe you are real," said Eirian. "If you want me to believe that you exist, you will have to prove it to me in some other way. I have wanted a sibling for years. How do I know you are not some dark part of my subconscious simply voicing my deepest desire?"

"Hah! Like you have a dark bone in your naive little body," laughed Tola. "The darkest thing you have ever done is hide your relationship with that *half-breed*," Tola spat the word. "That, by the way, is your deepest desire, to be allowed to be with your precious Elior. Your desire for a sibling comes second to that."

"The fact that you know about Elior and me only makes me believe all the more that you are a figment of my imagination," a defiant gleam shone in Eirian's eye. "I will still require more proof if I am to believe you."

Fierce Anger flashed in Tola's eyes and Eirian's blood ran cold with fear. The anger quickly vanished, replaced immediately with confidence.

"Very well," said Tola, a dangerous edge to her voice. "If it is proof you desire, then proof you shall have. But remember, Princess," Tola reached out one long arm and cupped Eirian's cheek with her hand, digging her black fingernails into Eirian's skin, "be careful what you ask for."

Tola vanished once again. Eirian's face burned where Tola scratched her. She ignored it, positive that the pain would be gone when she woke up. She sat down in the dirt and waited for the trees to surround her. This time, however, the trees stayed where they were. She tried closing her eyes and opening them again, but nothing happened. She stood up and walked around the clearing and then eventually, down the narrow path that wove between the trees.

"Wake up," she ordered herself. "Wake up!"

Eirian walked for hours. Her eyelids grew heavy. Exhausted, she yawned and laid down in the middle of the path, falling into a restless sleep.

She woke with a start in her own bed, tangled in the silken sheets and soaked with a cold sweat. Her cheek burned with a dull, fading ache. She rubbed the spot with her fingers and could not feel a wound, but she checked the mirror just to be sure. She breathed a sigh of relief as she saw only clear white skin.

She briefly thought about telling her parents about her dreams, but decided against it. She did not want to say anything that might detract from the excitement of their new arrival. The thought made Eirian smile. Children were rare gifts in her world and always celebrated, from the poorest beggar woman living on the street to the High Queen in her glistening, crystalline castle.

After breakfast, Eirian told her tutor that she would prefer to have a day of free study in the palace's extensive and ornate library, filled with plush armchairs and large tables with bright, silver lamps in the center, rather than whatever lesson he had planned. She examined the endless rows of oak shelves, loading her arms with any book that appeared slightly helpful. She lugged them all to her favorite window-lined corner, and pored over them, scanning each page for the name "Tola." Eirian knew she had heard that name before. She needed to remember where before she went to bed that night. Eirian asked for more proof simply as a way to stall for time until she figured out why she recognized the name.

"I thought I'd find you back here." Elior's voice broke through the words of Eirian's current book, drawing her back to reality.

She looked up. Elior held a tray with a pot of fragrant tea and a large pile of sandwiches.

"Were you looking for me, or did you run into Alyia and she told you where I was?" Eirian cleared off a spot on the table for Elior to put down the tray.

"Both," he answered. "I hadn't seen you all morning, and Alyia said that you missed lunch. I volunteered to bring this to you." He put the tray on the table and sat down in the chair opposite her.

"I missed lunch?" asked Eirian. She poured tea into two cups and passed one to Elior.

"Yes, you missed lunch," repeated Elior. "What is it that has so consumed your attention?"

Eirian looked around to make sure they were alone and leaned over the table to prevent anyone from listening in.

"Have you ever heard of anyone named Tola?" she asked.

"Tola?" Elior sat back in his chair. "It does sound familiar, like a character from a childhood story."

"Exactly," nodded Eirian. "Only I cannot remember which one." She gestured to the piles of storybooks.

"We could ask my mother," suggested Elior. "I'm sure she'd know."

"No," Eirian shook her head. "We cannot tell anyone. Not yet." She winced. The burning in her cheek grew stronger.

"Why not?" asked Elior. "I mean, it's just a story. I don't think there's –" Elior's words cut off as he leaned over and took Eirian's face in his hands. "What happened to your cheek?"

Eirian pulled away and clapped a hand over the side of her face. She stood and rushed to the nearest mirror. Slowly, cautiously, she pulled her hand away. Swollen, angry red scratch marks, absent that morning, now covered Eirian's left cheek.

"No, Elior." Eirian turned to Elior, stunned. "Tola is not just a story. She is real."

Elior and Eirian tended to her cheek, then went back to the library. They scoured the books, hoping to find out more about the woman in Eirian's dreams.

"I think I found it." Elior jumped from his chair, triumphantly holding aloft an old storybook.

He dragged his chair around to Eirian's side of the table and set down the ancient storybook. He leaned in close. Most of the stories in the book had either been retold often enough that they were unrecognizable from the originals or entirely forgotten. The title of the story that Elior pointed out read, "The Razor Wood," but it was the picture beneath it that drew Eirian's attention. A woman, with red hair trailing behind her, wearing a forest green dress, stood in a black forest while a young girl in a white dress cried at her feet.

"That is her," whispered a trembling Eirian. "That is Tola, and that is the forest from my dream."

The story spoke of a young maiden whose lover had died in battle. She went to Tola to beg her to bring him back. Tola agreed to help, but warned that the price for her request would be steep. The maiden agreed to give anything and struck the deal. The maiden left the forest and found her lover waiting for her. She was overjoyed until she returned home and discovered the price for his life: the loss of her dear father. The maiden went back to the Razor Wood to find Tola. The story ended with Tola bringing back the maiden's father, but taking the maiden's life instead.

"Well, that was depressing." Elior looked up from the book.

"Indeed." Eirian stared at the picture in the open book. "What does Tola want with me?"

"Maybe she thinks you want to make a deal with her?"

"Not if the price is that steep," Eirian shook her head. "I love you, Elior, but I would rather find a way for us to be together on our own than go to that witch for help."

"I agree." Elior put an arm around Eirian and she leaned her head on his shoulder. "If she comes back, then you need to tell her that. Don't let her take charge of the conversation. You are the future queen. Use that to your advantage."

Eirian nodded.

"And if that doesn't work, then you should tell your father," continued Elior. "He's the king. He'll know what to do."

Eirian sighed. "I hope it does not come to that. Daddy already has much on his mind. I do not wish to worry him further."

"Eirian? Are you still in here?"

Elior released Eirian at the sound of King Alberic's voice. Eirian quickly turned the book to a different story as the king came around one of the bookshelves. Elior and Eirian stood.

"Yes, Daddy." Eirian gestured to the books littering the table. "Elior and I were just looking through some old storybooks. I want to be ready with plenty of bedtime stories for when the baby comes."

"Ah! That is your secret assignment for the day." Alberic smiled. "Your mother and I were beginning to get concerned."

"There is nothing to be concerned about, Daddy," lied Eirian.

She stepped forward and Alberic noticed the bandage on her cheek.

"What happened here?" he asked, tilting her face to the side to examine it.

"Nothing." Eirian tried to think of an excuse. "I was reaching for a book on a high shelf and slipped. I cut my face on the corner of the shelf. Elior said we should tell you, but it is such a small cut, I did not want to worry you."

Alberic looked at her for another moment. Eirian offered him a reassuring smile, hoping he did not see through her dishonesty.

"Very well." He nodded and released her. "I will let the two of you get back to your assignment." He kissed Eirian on her uninjured cheek.

Elior bowed his head as Alberic left. Eirian waited until Alberic was out of earshot, then collapsed back into her chair.

"Do you think I should have told him the truth?" she asked.

"I can't answer that." Elior stood behind her and tenderly rubbed her shoulders. "However, I can tell you that if you don't think this is important enough to tell your parents about, then you probably shouldn't let it bother you this much."

Eirian leaned into Elior's touch. "I will give it a little more time. If I cannot figure out what Tola wants on my own, then I will ask my father for help, but not today."

"If that's what you think is best." Elior kissed the top of her head. "Now, that bedtime story idea is not a bad one." He sat back in his chair and picked up a different book. "What do you say?"

Eirian smiled and pulled the book closer so they could share. They spent the rest of the day choosing their favorite stories to read to the baby.

Hidden Identity

3

The pain in Eirian's cheek steadily increased throughout the night. She retired to her room after dinner, her cheek on fire. She shut the door and rushed to her mirror, tearing the bandage from her face. Bright red skin throbbed around black, discolored gashes oozing milky fluid. Eirian gagged at the stench of death emanating from the scratches. She barely made it to her wash basin before her stomach emptied itself of its contents.

"Now do you believe I am real?" asked Tola from behind her.

Eirian spun around and, all at once, again stood in the Razor Wood. She opened her mouth to answer, but another wave of nausea trapped the words in her throat. She imagined the skin around her wound dissolving and spreading across her body until nothing remained except muscle and bone. Unbearable pain drove all coherent thought from her mind. Nothing existed except the fire on her skin.

"The sap from these trees is incredibly toxic, but it does make a lovely nail color." Tola held out a hand, palm down. "Do you not agree?"

Eirian's vision blurred and she sank to her knees.

"Why are you doing this?" she managed to ask through gritted teeth.

"You said you wanted proof that I existed. Here is your proof." Tola crouched to Eirian's level. She cocked her head to one side and raised a condescending eyebrow. "Do you believe me?"

Eirian nodded. Her head swam and she squeezed her eyes shut.

"Good." Tola forced Eirian's head back by grabbing a fistful of Eirian's hair from the back of her head, winding long fingers around strands of colorless locks, holding her in place, helpless.

Tola produced a vial from thin air and poured the foul-tasting concoction down Eirian's throat. The pain Instantly vanished. Eirian touched her cheek and found no sign of the scratches. She looked up at Tola in confusion.

"Well, I cannot have you dying before we have discussed our business," said Tola, in a matter-of-fact tone of voice. "What good would that do me? Rise."

Eirian stood. "I will not make a deal with you, Tola." She straightened as much as possible. "I do not need, nor do I want, your help."

Tola laughed, a clear, high sound that echoed inside Eirian's head.

"Dear child, I am not here to make a deal with *you*," she dramatically wiped at the corners of her eyes. "I am here to discuss payment for a deal already made."

"I have never made a deal with you." Eirian frowned. Her eyebrows knit together in confusion.

"No, of course not," Tola smirked, "but your father has."

"No." Eirian shook her head in disbelief. "No, you are lying."

"I thought we previously established that I am not lying."

"My parents do not keep secrets from me," insisted Eirian.

"Always so sure of everything," sighed Tola. "The arrogancy of elves make me sick. Ask your father, if you doubt me. When you do, tell him I said, 'hello.'" A sly smile played on Tola's lips. "I am sure that hearing from me after two centuries will bring back all sorts of memories."

"What was the deal?" asked Eirian after a pause.

Tola's smile grew. "I am glad you asked. Especially since it involves you."

Tola waved her hand and two dark brown, wooden chairs grew out of the ground. She sat down in one and offered the other to Eirian.

"I think I prefer to stand." Eirian warily eyed the chair. They did not appear to be made of the same wood as the trees, but she would not take the chance.

"Suit yourself." Tola shrugged. She smoothed the front of her blood-red dress and began speaking in a story teller's voice. "Just over two hundred years ago, King Alberic and Queen Livia became parents to a lovely baby girl. The whole kingdom rejoiced with them. However, the baby was terribly ill. Even the court healer could not discover the cause of her illness. The king and queen were afraid they would lose their new little bundle of joy." Tola sniffled and pretended to wipe away a tear.

Eirian knew that she was sick as a baby. Her mother often told her it was a miracle she survived.

"Fearing he had no other choice, King Alberic payed me a visit," continued Tola. "He wanted me to make the child well. He said he would pay any price necessary." Tola giggled. "I love hearing those words. In any case, he signed the contract without even reading it first."

Eirian's confidant demeanor slipped. Her father always read every contract through twice, and made his advisors read them over once each before signing anything. He never wanted to be caught off guard by any hidden clauses. Perhaps she now knew why.

"Do you want to sit down now, Dear?" asked Tola. "You seem a little pale." She chuckled at her own joke.

Eirian composed herself, ignoring Tola's offer to sit. "What was the price?" she asked.

Tola sighed and rolled her eyes. "What have I told you about being patient? I already told you, we will get to everything in time. I need to finish my story first. Now, where was I?" Tola tapped her chin with one finger. "Oh, yes! King Alberic signed the contract without reading it. I told him that he would return home to find the baby miraculously healed. He did not even ask about the price. All he asked was that I promise not to tell the queen, which was an easy enough request."

Tola fell silent. Eirian waited for her to continue, but Tola seemed to be waiting for Eirian to respond.

"How do I know you are not lying to me?" asked Eirian.

Tola grinned. "I still have the contract, if you would like to see it."

The faerie stood, produced a scroll with the wave of her hand and unrolled it with a flourish. Eirian tried to read it, but Tola directed her attention to the bottom where Eirian saw, clear as day, her father's signature.

"You see?" Tola turned the scroll to prevent Eirian from reading anything more. "'This contract stands as a lasting agreement between King Alberic of Varia and Tola of The Razor Wood for services provided to the first party by the second party,'" read Tola. "'The first party hereby agrees to the price set forth by the second party for the following service...' blah, blah, blah, etcetera, etcetera, etcetera." Tola rolled up the scroll.

"What was the price?" asked Eirian. She recalled the story she and Elior read earlier. The price for one life was another life. Eirian's stomach churned; she knew whose life Tola wanted.

"You are a smart girl. See if you can figure it out. Until next time, Princess." Tola blew a kiss in Eirian's direction. She vanished into thin air.

Eirian found herself back in her bedroom, lying on the floor in front of her mirror, her body stiff and sore. The sun shone through her window, and birds sang in the garden beyond.

"Princess? Are you awake?" asked Alyia, peeking through the door. Alyia's eyes widened and she rushed to Eirian's side. "Princess? Are you alright? What happened?" She helped Eirian to her feet.

"I—" Eirian tried to think of an excuse that would not cause Alyia to worry. "I—I do not know." She sighed and rubbed her temples.

"I'll go fetch the queen." Alyia ran out of the room before Eirian could stop her.

Eirian sat down on her bed and tried, again, to think of some believable reason for waking up on the floor. Alyia returned, followed by the king and queen. Eirian sighed, she had no excuse. She claimed that she fell out of bed and told her parents not to worry. They left her, telling her to let them know if it happened again. Alberic paused at the door and turned back.

"Are you sure there is nothing more going on?" he asked.

Eirian shook her head and smiled. "No, Daddy. There is nothing to be concerned about."

King Alberic lingered a moment longer, turned, and left.

Eirian went to find Elior after breakfast. She wanted to go sooner, but missing breakfast may have aroused her parents' suspicion.

"Did you find out what Tola wants?" asked Elior. The two sat in the safety of their old playhouse.

"I believe so." Eirian told Elior about her most recent conversation with Tola. "Elior, I think she wants the baby."

Elior stiffened.

"What makes you think that?"

"A life for a life," explained Eirian. "She saved mine when I was a baby and now, she returns just as my mother is pregnant again. What else could it be?"

"Come on." Elior took Eirian's hand and pulled her to the door. "You need to tell your parents about this. Now."

"No." Eirian pulled away. "I do not want to worry them."

"Eirian, this is too big for the two of us."

"I do not even know for sure if I am right. What if I am wrong? I would have made my parents worry for nothing." Eirian chewed her bottom lip.

"Not for nothing. Even if she doesn't want the baby, she obviously wants something." Elior leaned closer and took her hand again. "Please, Eirian."

Eirian leaned into him.

"Okay. You are right, Elior. This is too big for us."

Elior sighed in relief and kissed her. "Let's go."

Hidden Identity

4

Eirian sat on a sofa in one of the parlors and waited for her parents. Elior stood beside her.

"It'll be okay," he reassured her. "Your parents will know what to do."

"I hope you are right," replied Eirian.

She reached for his hand but pulled away when the door opened. She felt the heat of a blush creep into her cheeks. She closed her eyes and took a deep breath to dispel the color from her face as her parents entered the room.

"You wanted to speak with us?" asked Livia.

She sat beside her daughter on the sofa. Elior bowed and started toward the door. Eirian, momentarily forgetting about her parents, grabbed his hand to stop him.

"Do not leave," she begged. "Please."

"You'll be fine." Elior glanced at the king and queen. "This is a family matter." He surreptitiously gave Eirian's hand a soft squeeze before leaving the room.

Alberic glanced at Livia, his expression unreadable, then turned to Eirian. "What is the matter, Dear?"

Eirian paused. "I do not know how to begin."

"You do not need to fear." Livia gently took Eirian's hand. "You can tell us anything."

Eirian took a deep breath, closing her eyes for a moment. "I met Tola."

Livia's grip on Eirian's hand tightened. Eirian opened her eyes to gauge her parents' reactions. Livia's eyes widened; her lips parted slightly in surprise. Alberic stood stiffer than usual, his expression impossible to read.

"What?" asked Livia in a near whisper. "How? When?"

"I have spoken to her several times," explained Eirian. "She appears to me in my dreams. The first time was about a fortnight ago. She told me that you were going to have a baby. I did not know who she was then. I did not know who she was until yesterday."

"That is what you were doing with the storybooks." Alberic sighed. "Eirian, Tola is very dangerous. Why did you not come to us about this sooner?"

"I did not wish to worry you," Eirian glanced at her lap. "As I said, I did not know who she was until yesterday, and then I wanted to wait until I discovered what she wanted."

"What does she want?" asked Livia.

Eirian glanced up at Alberic. "Payment. For the deal you made with her when I was a baby."

Alberic paled and he sank into the nearest chair.

"Alberic," Livia's voice trembled, "tell me this is not true. Tell me you did not go to Tola."

Alberic remained silent, one fist pressed against his mouth.

"You promised me you would not go to her," continued Livia. "We agreed we would find another way."

"What choice did I have?" asked Alberic, his voice thick with emotion. "Eirian was dying! Nothing else was working! Tola gave her back to us! If I had not gone to see her—" Alberic's voice cracked on the last word. He paused, composed himself, and continued. "If I had not gone to see her, then Eirian would not be here."

Tears filled Eirian's eyes. No one spoke.

"What was the price?" asked Livia, breaking the silence.

"I do not know," admitted Alberic. "I was too concerned about Eirian to ask. I did not think there was a price too steep for our daughter's life."

"So, you made a deal with Tola without knowing what you were agreeing to?" Livia's voice held an even tone, her emotions barely concealed.

Alberic nodded. "Now she has returned, demanding payment, and I do not even know what that payment is."

"I think I know what it is," Eirian spoke up. Her parents looked at her. "I do not know for sure, but I have a feeling she wants the baby."

Livia gasped. Her hand protectively covered her belly.

"It is the only thing that makes sense," continued Eirian. "Why else would she wait until now to come forward?"

"I want to know why she came to you in the first place." Alberic shook his head. "I am the one who made the deal with her."

"We may never know why she decided to go to Eirian. Perhaps because it was Eirian's life in the balance." Livia lifted her chin. "Right now, we need to decide what we are going to do. It is true that we do not know for sure that Tola wants the baby, but we do need to prepare for that possibility, and how we are going to prevent it."

"We need to get you and Eirian out of the palace," Alberic anxiously rubbed his fingers together, "somewhere Tola will not be able to find you while I figure out what she wants, and, if it is the baby, find a way out of the deal without putting Eirian's life in danger."

"But she can enter my dreams." Eirian looked from her father to her mother. "Will she not be able to find me that way?"

"No, even her magic has limits." Livia placed a comforting hand on Eirian's arm. "She still needs to know where someone is before she can enter their dreams."

Alberic rubbed his chin in thought. "The Winter Palace. No one else knows where it is. You will go with a minimal number of servants. I will remain here."

"I do not wish to go without you." Livia reached for her husband. "What if she does manage to find us there? I do not want to face her alone."

"I will send some guards with you," assured Alberic. He gently covered Livia's hand with his. "If Tola does show, they can hold her off until I arrive."

"I want Elior to go, too," added Eirian. "He is my best friend, and, if you cannot be there with us, he is the only other person with whom I will feel safe."

"That is a fair request," smiled Livia. "Do you agree, Alberic?"

"Yes." Alberic nodded. "Elior is brave and strong, and it is clear he is loyal to Eirian. He will not allow any harm to come to either of you."

Eirian smiled and hugged her father.

"Thank you, Daddy. I apologize for not coming to you sooner with this."

"I accept your apology." Alberic returned Eirian's hug. "Now, go and pack. You will leave tonight."

Eirian kissed her father and left the room. She overheard her parents talking as she walked away.

"I still do not like this plan, Alberic."

"Nor do I, my love, but, at the moment, I cannot think of a better one."

Elior waited just outside the room. He fell into step beside Eirian as she walked down the hall.

"I assume you overheard?" asked Eirian.

Elior nodded. "I wasn't trying to eavesdrop, but yes, I heard the plan. Do you think it will be enough?"

"I hope so." Eirian stopped walking and turned to him. "I am afraid, Elior."

He pulled her close.

"You heard what your father said. He'll be here trying to find a way to stop her," Elior pulled away and faced her, "and I will be there with you. Everything will be fine. Now, go pack. I'm sure King Alberic will send for me soon."

Eirian nodded and hugged him once more. She wanted to kiss him, but they were too exposed standing in the middle of the corridor.

Eirian stood between her parents outside the castle and glanced up at the full moon, drawing comfort from its soft, reflective glow. Elior and another servant tightened harnesses around two horses and secured them to a carriage. Eirian rubbed her arms, warming them against the cool air. Devin – Captain of the Guard, and Claudette's husband – helped Alyia into the carriage, followed by Livia's lady-in-waiting, Larissa. Alberic sent one carriage – filled with luggage and servants, including Claudette and her daughter – earlier in the night.

Devin turned to the royal family. "We're ready, Your Majesties."

"Good bye, my love." Livia tenderly placed a hand on Alberic's arm.

Alberic caressed her cheek. "We will be together again soon."

Livia closed her eyes and leaned into his touch, covering his hand with her own. She lingered, unwilling to break away. In a rare public display of affection, she turned and pressed a kiss to Alberic's palm. Reluctantly, she pulled back and allowed Devin to help her into the carriage.

Eirian wrapped her arms around her father and held him tight. "Send for us soon, please."

Alberic kissed Eirian on the cheek. "I will try my very hardest," he promised. "In the meantime, stay safe."

Eirian brushed her hand against Elior's as Devin helped her into the carriage. Devin glanced at the young elves as he closed the carriage door.

"Elior, you sit up here with me, next to the driver," he said. "Let the ladies have their privacy."

"Yes, Sir." Elior climbed up onto the bench at the front of the carriage.

Alberic turned to the driver. "Remember, drive straight to the Winter Palace. Do not stop, save to change horses at the previously discussed locations."

"Yes, Your Majesty." The driver bowed his head and snapped the reigns.

The carriage moved forward with a lurch. Eirian turned and stared out the back window, watching her father fade into the darkness. When she could no longer see him, she turned back around.

Livia reached across and put a hand on Eirian's knee. "We will be fine, Eirian. There is no need to cry." She gave Eirian a comforting smile, but Eirian saw tears in her mother's eyes.

Eirian sniffled. "I feel like this is my fault. If I had told you and Daddy about my dreams sooner, then maybe we could have come up with a different plan."

Livia dried Eirian's eyes with a blue handkerchief. "I do not think it would have changed things. Alberic needs to stay behind. The queen and princess may leave unexpectedly and without reason, but a king has responsibilities."

"I know," sighed Eirian. "I just wish none of this had happened."

"As do I, dear." Livia leaned back and stared out her window. "As do I."

The gentle sway of the of the cart along the dirt road and the lullaby of nocturnal insects transformed the carriage into a cradle. Eirian's eyelids grew heavy. She shook the sleep from her mind and pinched herself to stay awake. She did not want to risk dreaming about Tola. She did not want Tola to find out their plan.

Eirian yawned and leaned against the carriage wall. "Maybe I will close my eyes, just for a moment."

She awoke the next morning to warm sun on her face and sprite laughter in the air. She sat up and stretched, her muscles tense and stiff from her unnatural sleeping position.

She rubbed her eyes. "How long was I asleep?"

"Most of the morning." Livia handed Eirian a covered dish. "How did you sleep?" From Livia's tone, Eirian knew what she really asked.

"Peacefully," she answered.

Livia relaxed with a soft sigh.

Eirian uncovered the dish containing her breakfast and bit into a piece of sweet fruit. She glanced out her window, staring at dryads and wood sprites playing in white barked trees.

"Mama?" Eirian turned to her mother. "Can we make a short stop? I need to—um—" Eirian gave her mother a look that she hoped would explain what she needed.

Livia nodded in understanding and ordered the driver to stop the carriage. Devin opened the door and helped Eirian down. Eirian stepped into the forest, just out of sight from the main road. Two curious sprites flew over to investigate. A dryad jumped down from her tree and hissed at the sprites, shooing them away. She bowed to Eirian, then knelt down and touched the ground. Thick green vines sprouted around Eirian, giving her a curtain of privacy.

Eirian thanked the dryad as she walked back to the carriage. The two curious sprites from before flew back to Eirian, carrying a blue daisy between them, heads hung in shame. They offered the daisy to Eirian.

"Thank you." Eirian accepted the flower and tucked it into her hair. "You are forgiven."

The sprites lifted their heads and grinned. They chittered a thank you and flew back into the forest. Elior, watching from his perch on the driver's bench, laughed at the exchange. Eirian smiled up at him and shook her head.

Devin helped Eirian back into the carriage. She looked back out the window as their journey continued. She compared the familiar, bustling White Forest, full of life and peace, to the cold lifelessness of the Razor Wood. She desperately hoped their plan worked. She did not want to spend another second in the foul Razor Wood, dream or not. More than anything, she did not want to see Tola ever again. She wanted to live in peace and comfort with her family, teaching her new sibling how to be a proper prince or princess.

Wishful thinking, I know.

Livia, as if sensing Eirian's thoughts, took Eirian's hand and gave it a gentle squeeze. Eirian smiled in thanks and relaxed.

Everything will be okay. Daddy will take care of everything.

Hidden Identity

5

Eirian laughed in relief at the sight of the Winter Palace's sturdy stone walls and strong towers. The smaller palace acted as both vacation home and fortress. The White Forest surrounded it on all sides, concealing it from unfriendly eyes. The carriage stopped outside the palace's double oak entrance doors where two uniformed guards stood at attention.

One guard stepped forward and gave Devin a salute. "Area secure, Captain. The palace is safe and everything is prepared for Queen Livia and Princess Eirian."

"Very good." Devin jumped from the driver's bench and opened the carriage door. He offered a hand to Livia. "Your Majesty."

Livia, followed by Larissa, Alyia, and Eirian, accepted Devin's assistance out of the carriage. Eirian snuck a goodnight glance at Elior, then followed her mother into the palace. Warm air, naturally supplied by the heat of thermal springs in several of the rooms, surrounded Eirian the moment she stepped through the doors. Claudette greeted them in the foyer.

"Welcome, Your Majesty, Your Highness." Claudette bowed her head to Livia and Eirian in turn. "Your luggage has already been brought to your rooms. Everything is prepared and ready for you. Dinner will be ready in two hours."

"Thank you, Claudette." Livia turned to Eirian. "I am going to my room for a time. I will see you at dinner."

Eirian nodded. She followed Alyia to her own room, and the connected hot spring bath. Eirian breathed in the scent of lilac and lavender bath oils. She disrobed and stepped into the warm, perfumed water, completely submerging herself into its comfortable depths. She imagined her worries washing away as easily as the grime from her two-day journey. Her stiff muscles loosened. She sat up and grabbed the soap, generously scrubbing it along her skin and through her hair.

I wish I could stay here forever, drowning my fears in lavender-scented water.

"Are you planning on staying in there until you become a mermaid, Miss?" Alyia asked, entering with a towel draped over one arm.

Eirian smiled and gave the water a small kick.

"Is that an option?" she asked, sinking deeper into the spring. "Because if it is, then my answer is yes."

"Come on now, Your Highness. Your mother is waiting for you in the dining hall." Alyia helped Eirian out of the spring and handed her the towel. "There's a gown ready on your bed."

The Winter Palace was much smaller than their main castle, but it still felt too large and empty for Eirian with most of the court absent. Eirian did not have any lessons to occupy her time, her tutor stayed behind. She spent her days sitting with her mother or taking long, romantic walks with Elior. They often walked hand-in-hand through the palace grounds without fear of getting caught by the reduced staff. Eirian relished the security of Elior's embrace, the comfort of his kisses. Their love kept her concerns at bay.

Eirian missed her father terribly. In the two centuries that she had been alive, she had never spent this long away from him. She could only imagine how her mother felt. Livia never showed her true feelings in front of others, but when they were alone, Eirian saw deep loneliness in the queen's eyes.

The growth of Livia's abdomen manifested the passage of time. In only a few months, Eirian saw the first evidence of her new sibling.

"I hope it is a girl," said Eirian one night while she and her mother sat in their favorite parlor.

The parlor contained a large painting of the royal family when Eirian was five years old. The artist captured the child-like gleam in Livia's eyes and the gentle gaze of her father while maintaining their regality. Little Eirian, on the other hand, watched a butterfly instead of looking at the artist. Livia told her once that they spent hours trying to get her to sit still.

"Why is that?" asked Livia.

"Because, I can give her all my old toys and show her my favorite places to play."

"You can do that if it is a boy, too," laughed Livia.

Eirian smiled at her mother. "I know. I just want a sister."

"I suppose Elior is enough of a brother to you. Is that it?"

Eirian laughed and nodded like she agreed. There were times she wanted to tell her parents how she and Elior really felt about each other, but she was afraid they would send him away. Not only did Elior not have a drop of royal blood in his veins, but he was also half human. Those two strikes were enough discount him from the list of possible suitors, no matter how much her parents liked him.

The months crawled by at a frustratingly slow pace. Spring gave way to Summer which, in turn, gave way to Autumn. The leaves in the surrounding forest changed from bright green to gold, yellow, and orange. A chill returned to the air.

Eirian and Elior leaned against each other in the north tower, enjoying some alone time and admiring the view of the, now colorful, White Forest stretching as far as the eye could see. Eirian glanced down and saw a man on horseback riding up the path to the palace. Eirian jumped up in excitement and took off down the stairs, leaving Elior to chase after her.

"Daddy!" yelled Eirian, running to greet her father.

Alberic's feet hardly touched the ground before Eirian threw her arms around him, nearly knocking him off balance.

"I missed you."

"I missed you too, Eirian." Alberic tenderly returned Eirian's hug.

He looked up, noticing Livia in the doorway.

"I was wondering when you would arrive." Livia brightly smiled.

Alberic let go of Eirian and turned to embrace his wife. "I am here now. There is no need to worry."

"Does this mean you found a way to stop Tola?" Eirian hopefully stepped toward her parents.

The smile faded from Alberic's face as he turned back to Eirian. "Not yet. I sent out men to see if they could find her, but they have all returned with negative reports."

"Oh," Eirian's face fell.

Alberic walked over and lifted her chin. "This does not mean I have given up. We will find a way to stop her. I promise."

"Eirian, your father has had a long journey and I am sure he wants to rest," said Livia.

Alberic kissed Eirian on the cheek and followed Livia into the palace, leaving Elior and Eirian alone. Eirian buried her face in Elior's shoulder and cried. She did not care if anyone saw them. Elior wrapped his arms around her and rubbed her back.

"I thought it was over," she choked out between sobs. "When I saw Daddy riding down the path, I thought, 'He did it. It is over. We can go home.'"

"Oh, Princess," the witch's voice filled the air, "you should have known better. It is not over until I say that it is over."

"You!" Eirian jumped back in surprise and horror. Tola's vile homeland replaced the courtyard. The dark, foreboding forest surrounded her, the ancient white tree was gone—as was Elior. "How did you? I thought—"

"You thought you were safe? Oh, my poor, poor child." Tola reached out a hand to caress Eirian's face. She backed away from the cold touch.

"Leave us alone!" screamed Eirian. "Just go away and leave us alone!"

"Not until I get what I came for," snapped Tola. "The king promised me his second daughter and his second daughter I shall have!"

"Why?" snapped Eirian. "What need do you have for a baby?"

Tola shook her head. "Not any baby. Your sister."

"No." Eirian straightened to her full height of nearly seven feet. "I will not let you have her."

"Do you honestly think you can stop me?" laughed Tola. "A child such as yourself standing against someone with my power. The thought is too ludicrous to even entertain."

"Laugh all you want, Tola, but remember, I am the future queen. It would be wise not to underestimate me." Eirian turned her back on Tola and started walking, intent on walking straight out of the wood.

"I *will* have that baby!" Tola shouted after her. "There is nowhere you can hide that I will not find you!"

Eirian did not look back. "Watch me."

A light appeared in front of her and she walked into it. A tingling caress washed over her. She closed her eyes and let the sensation take her away. The light faded and she opened her eyes. A triumphant smile touched her lips. She lay in her own bed, staring into the concerned faces of Elior and Alyia.

"Thank goodness, you're awake, Your Highness!" exclaimed Alyia.

Eirian blinked and rubbed her eyes. "What happened?"

"I was about to ask you the same thing. You passed out in my arms. I called for help immediately." Elior put a hand on her arm. "I—we were worried."

Eirian sat up and looked around the empty room. "Where are Mama and Daddy?"

"Your father was here for a while," said Elior, "but the queen went into labor an hour or so after I found you, and—"

"What?" Eirian threw off the blankets and ran down the hall to her parents' room. She saw a crescent moon outside as she ran past a window. Eirian, pre-occupied with her most recent dream, nearly ran into her father as he came through a door in front of her.

"Eirian!" he exclaimed, wrapping his arms around her. "You are alright."

"Elior said that Mama is in labor." Eirian pulled back.

Alberic smiled. "Not anymore. I was just on my way to check on you, and, if you were awake, bring you to meet your new sister."

Alberic led Eirian into the room. Livia – hair wet with sweat, but smiling – sat in her bed, propped up with several large pillows, nursing a peacefully content newborn. Anya, the midwife, stood off to the side with her assistant.

"Eirian," sighed Livia. "You are awake."

Eirian walked over to the bedside and looked at the tiny form in her mother's arms.

Livia smiled and carefully moved her arms to give Eirian a better view of the newborn. "Eirian, meet your baby sister, Aubree."

"Aubree," whispered Eirian in amazement.

She gently touched the soft white fuzz that covered the baby's head. Aubree stopped suckling and looked up at Eirian, her silver eyes locking onto Eirian's.

"She is beautiful," whispered Eirian in awe.

"Yes, she is," agreed Alberic, standing behind her.

"I promise I will not let anything happen to you, Aubree," said Eirian. "I will protect you with everything in me. I swear it."

Aubree wrapped her tiny hand around one of Eirian's fingers and smiled as if she understood what Eirian said. Eirian smiled. *Perhaps she had - babies are capable of far more than people usually give them credit for.* Eirian finally looked away from Aubree and turned to her father.

"Can I speak with you?" she asked. "It is important."

"Did she return?" asked Livia.

Eirian nodded. "I do not want to ruin this moment, but I also do not want to wait until it is too late."

Alberic nodded in understanding.

"That will be all, Anya," he said to the midwife. "We will send for you if we need you."

Anya bowed her head. "I will be just outside." She and her assistant backed out of the room.

Alberic turned to Eirian. "Now, tell us what happened."

Eirian told them about her recent encounter with Tola. She reached the part about Tola confirming that she was after the baby. Livia held Aubree tighter. Alberic paced.

"What are we going to do, Daddy?" asked Eirian when she finished her story. "We cannot let her have Aubree."

"No," agreed Alberic. "She will not have her."

"What does she want with her?" asked Livia. "What could she possibly want with our baby?"

Alberic shook his head. "Nothing good."

"We need to hide her. Take her and go somewhere. Just us." Eirian's eyes filled with tears; she could not include Elior in her plan. "We leave tonight. We do not tell anyone where we are going."

Livia sighed in exhaustion. "We cannot keep running and hiding forever. We tried that already and she still found us."

Alberic nodded in sympathy. "Eirian is right, nonetheless. Keeping Aubree safe is our number one priority. The problem lies in trying to find a place within the realm where—"

"That is it!" exclaimed Eirian. Her parents looked at her. "You said, 'a place within the realm.' If we take Aubree outside the realm, to the Mortal Realm, then she will be safe, right? The Veil would prevent Tola from using her magic, even if she did find us. Not even she is that powerful."

"The Mortal Realm is dangerous," said Livia. "It is filled with exiles and run-aways."

"Exiles and run-aways are nothing compared to Tola." Eirian shook off the memory of her most recent encounter with the witch. "Bringing Aubree there will give us more time to think of a plan."

Alberic thoughtfully nodded. "That does make sense. Unfortunately, as with coming here, we cannot all go.

Many of the exiles were banished by my hand. They will be sure to recognize me, even wearing human glamour. The same goes for you, Livia. As the queen, your face is widely known. Eirian, however, is still very young, and she has never left the kingdom."

"Alberic, what are you suggesting?" Livia stared at her husband with her head tilted slightly to the side.

"I am suggesting that Eirian take Aubree to the Mortal Realm. Alone."

"No!" exclaimed Eirian as Alberic's words sank in. "I cannot go alone! Do not make me go alone, Daddy! Please!"

Aubree started crying and Livia held her close to calm her. She quieted and Alberic spoke again.

"I know this is a frightening proposition," he put a hand on Eirian's shoulder, "but I also know that if your mother and I joined you in the Mortal Realm, we would be found at once. Many exiles worked for Tola in the past and would alert her to our presence there. Even without her magic, Tola is still cunning, and we would be outnumbered. If you take her yourself, then Livia and I will be able to keep your location a secret, and you will both be safe."

"But –" began Eirian, tears rolling down her cheeks.

Alberic wiped them away.

"Eirian, there is no one I trust more for this mission." Tears gleamed in his own eyes. "I believe in you. You are strong. You proved that to me by standing up to Tola. Many, including myself, I admit, can only cower in front of her."

"Your father speaks the truth." Livia held out a hand. Eirian stepped forward and took it. "You are stronger than you know. I am proud of the woman you have become."

Eirian wanted to argue more, but as she stared down at her sister, tiny and helpless, she knew that she was the only one who could protect her.

"When do I leave?" she asked.

Hidden Identity

6

Eirian sat on a stone bench in the courtyard, facing a decorative white tree. The words she wanted to tell Elior raced through her mind, things she knew she could not say. In order to throw Tola off the scent, only King Alberic, Queen Livia, Claudette – in the role of Aubree's wet-nurse – Devin, and Eirian knew about the plan. Eirian avoided Elior; she knew she would not be able to control her emotions if she saw him.

"Eirian?" came Elior's voice behind her.

She did not turn around. She focused all her attention on not bursting into tears.

"I've been looking everywhere for you." He sat down on the bench beside her. "What happened?"

Eirian shook her head and turned away from him.

"Eirian, you're scaring me." Elior put a tender hand on Eirian's back. "What's going on? Did Tola come back?"

"I cannot say."

"Why not?" asked Elior. "You always tell me everything. Why can't you—"

"Elior, please," Eirian cut him off. "I cannot say. Please do not make me." She closed her eyes to hold back the tears.

"Eirian," began Elior.

Eirian turned and kissed him. She did not care if anyone saw. She wrapped her arms around his neck and kissed him like she would never see him again.

"That felt like a goodbye kiss," whispered Elior when she pulled away. "Now I'm really worried."

Afraid she would break down and tell him everything or worse, change her mind, Eirian ran out of the courtyard. She ran to her room and collapsed on the bed, sobbing. For the third time that day, she ran away from him.

She sat up and wiped her eyes, her tears spent. She went to a gray marble wash basin beside her vanity and splashed cold water on her face to ease her puffy, red eyes. She took a deep, steadying breath.

"I am Eirian, Princess of Varia." She spoke to herself aloud and with conviction. "I must do my duty to protect my sister, regardless of the people I leave behind. I am strong. I can do this."

She opened her wardrobe, running her hand along the soft materials of her many elegant dresses until she found the one she wanted; a simple, off-white evening gown adorned with a navy sash and trim. The dress reminded her of the illustration in the story about Tola. She pushed that thought aside and put it on.

She sat at her dressing table and let her silver hair loose. She stared into the mirror, memorizing the sharp edges and delicate pointed ears of her Elvish features.

How long will it be before I see this face again? she wondered.

She brushed her hair till it shone and finished with a simple braid that hung over her shoulder. She picked up a silver headpiece studded with light blue gems, the one she always wore. She carefully placed the clear sign of royalty on her pillow. She would not need it. She removed her ring, which bore the royal seal, and placed it with her headpiece on her pillow. She went over to her jewelry box and sifted through the piles of bracelets and rings and necklaces, all made from precious metals and studded with gemstones—any one of them could give away her secret. Her fingers closed around the one thing she could not bear to leave behind, a leather cord necklace with a butterfly carved from stone, the first birthday gift Elior gave her after their secret courtship began. Elior made it himself; the most treasured of all Eirian's possessions. She fastened on the necklace and went back down to the courtyard, relieved to find it empty.

Her parents arrived shortly, along with Claudette, Devin, and their two-year old daughter Marcia. Alberic tasked Devin with heading the search for Tola; he would not accompany them. Devin stood off to the side, saying goodbye to Claudette and Marcia.

"Are you ready?" asked Alberic.

"As ready as I can be," replied Eirian.

Alberic embraced Eirian and held her tight. "We will be together again soon."

Eirian nodded. "I know. I promise to take care of Aubree."

"I know you will." Alberic kissed her cheek and Eirian went to say goodbye to her mother.

"Be safe," said Livia. "Both of you."

"We will." Eirian hugged her mother, being careful of Aubree. "Mama? Will you give this to Elior, after we leave?" She put an envelope into Livia's hand.

"Of course, I will." Livia nodded. She looked down at the baby and kissed her on the head. "Do not be afraid, little one, I am putting you in the best hands."

She handed Aubree to Alberic for him to say goodbye.

"Your sister is brave and strong. She will keep you safe." Alberic kissed the baby and then handed her to Eirian. "Claudette knows a place where you can stay," he told her. "Remember, tell no one who you are. Do not use your real name. You may use Aubree's name because no one else knows it. Do not –" the words caught in his throat. He swallowed and tried again. "Do not try to contact us, it is not safe. When Tola is defeated, we will send for you. Hopefully it will not be long."

Eirian nodded in understanding.

Alberic lingered a moment longer. He stood up straight, his face an emotionless mask. "Well, if I wait any longer, I believe I shall lose my resolve."

He closed his eyes and summoned a shimmering gate in the invisible Veil that separated the Faerie Realm from the Mortal Realm. The iridescent metal gate easily swung open at Alberic's touch, revealing a hazy, unfocused preview of the world beyond.

Claudette bowed to the king and queen, took a last, long look at her husband, and stepped through the gate. Eirian said one more goodbye to her parents, turned, and followed Claudette. A mortal glamour covered her body, a human disguise that dulled her senses. She winced at the sudden loss of her faerie eyesight and hearing. Aubree fussed in her arms. The quiet, peaceful courtyard disappeared, replaced by a strange world with new sights, sounds, and smells. The sensations overwhelmed Eirian. She stood, transfixed, staring at the fascinating world around her. The mortal city was full of life despite the late hour. Mortals hurried past, barely glancing at the elves. Strange, swift moving boxes with people inside sped down a black road.

Cars. Eirian remembered from her Mortal Realm studies. *Though it seems my school books are outdated. These sleek cars look nothing like the square vehicles in the illustrations I studied.*

Brightly lit buildings lined the other side of the street. Eirian looked at a nearby sign. She stared at the strange letters until they formed a word in her mind.

Westin Park. That must be where we are.

Claudette gently touched her arm. Eirian jumped.

"This way." Claudette indicated the direction with a nod.

Eirian pulled Aubree closer and followed the older Elf down the street.

"When we get to the apartment, that is, the place where we are going to stay, my sister Charity will explain mortals themselves." Claudette readjusted her hold on her sleeping daughter. "I am still confused by most of what Charity tells me about them."

Charity chose to live in the mortal world. King Alberic gave his permission for them to visit each other on occasion. They would stay in Charity's apartment until they found a permanent residence. Eirian did not learn the term "apartment" in her lessons, but she did not bother asking how it differed from a house. She would find out soon enough.

Eirian yelped at a loud honking sound from one of the cars. "The Mortal Realm is very different from what my lessons described."

Claudette chuckled. "You will get used to it."

"You are sure Charity will not be angry that we are showing up unexpectedly?" Eirian stepped out of the path of a male mortal speaking into a small box pressed to his ear.

"A communication device called a cell phone," explained Claudette at Eirian's confused reaction to the device. "I know my sister well. She chose the name 'Charity' when she came here, for a reason. She will welcome us in with open arms and hot cups of tea."

Claudette led them to a large square building with a glass door. The older Elf scanned a button-filled panel beside the door. Eirian saw names written in a strange, mortal script, beside each button.

"Do not be afraid. Mortals have their own kind of magic, though they do not call it that." Claudette pushed the button beside her sister's name.

Eirian jumped as a voice came out of a grated place near the bottom of the panel.

"Yes?" asked the voice in mortal English. Eirian recognized the language from her lessons.

"Charity, it is Claudette," said Claudette in English. "I am sorry for the late hour, but I need your help. I am here with a young woman and we need a place to stay."

"Of course!" said Charity. "Come on up."

The door buzzed and clicked. Claudette pulled it open and stepped inside. Eirian followed, Aubree clutched to her chest. They entered a small, brightly colored room, with two empty doorways in the wall across from them. Signs indicated the purpose of the rooms: *Stairs* and *Laundry Room*. A shiny, silver, metal wall separated the doors. A panel with a single button and an engraved arrow sat to the right of the silver wall. Eirian wanted to stay and study the room, but Claudette guided her towards the doorway labeled "stairs."

"I do not want to frighten you more than necessary by taking the elevator," she said, again speaking Elvish, and nodded to the silver section of the wall.

"Elevator?" Eirian tilted her head to one side.

Claudette paused with one hand on the guardrail and one foot on the first step. "An elevator is like a tiny room that moves up and down on its own. Charity has tried to explain how it works many times, but, as I understand it, it is held in place by cords of twisted wire."

"How does it move?" asked Eirian.

"That is the part I do not understand," admitted Claudette.

She started walking up the stairs. Strange lamps hung on the stairwell walls.

"How do the lamps work without candles or fire?" Eirian leaned closer to a lamp, a hand outstretched.

Claudette gently grabbed Eirian's wrist, preventing her from touching the glowing bulb.

"Did you not learn about electricity in your lessons?"

Eirian tilted her head in thought. "Is that the power mortals gained when they learned how to capture and harness lightning?"

"More or less." Claudette continued up the stairs.

Eirian paused on the next landing and glanced down an empty doorway through which she saw a hallway lined with doors. She remembered the panel with names from outside.

She turned to Claudette. "Do each of these doors lead to someone's room?"

"Not quite." Claudette did not stop walking. "Entire families can live in a single apartment."

They climbed to the sixth floor of the building. Claudette entered the hallway and walked down to one of the doors. Charity stood in the doorway, waiting for them. She embraced her sister, kissed her sleeping niece on the forehead, and then turned to Eirian.

"And who do we have here?" asked Charity in Elvish.

Eirian opened her mouth to respond, but Claudette stopped her. She ushered everyone inside and securely locked the door before handing an envelope to Charity.

"What's this?" asked Charity.

"It is a letter from King Alberic explaining everything," said Claudette. "You are to read it and then burn it. Lives are at stake."

Charity nodded in understanding.

"Please, make yourself at home," she said to Eirian.

Eirian forced a smiled and nodded as she looked around the room.

I see! An apartment is a small house inside a large building. All those other doors must be other small houses! Eirian's forced smile became genuine, pleased that she solved the mystery.

Charity's small house contained a kitchen, dining area, and living area all combined into one. She wandered down the hallway and found a small washroom and two bedrooms. A mirror hung in the hall and Eirian paused in front of it. She stared at her new, human, reflection in wonder. She reached up and touched the pale, yellow hair where once sat silver locks. Small gray eyes set into a soft, pink face, blinked back at her. She moved aside some of her hair to see her new, rounded ears. She glanced down at her sister sound asleep in her arms. She looked almost the same as she had before, except for the fact that her ears were round now as well. Eirian wandered back to the living room as Charity finished reading the letter.

"Well, now that is some story." Charity walked into the kitchen and dug around in a drawer. She pulled out a small rectangular box, slid her finger across a wheel at the top and fire came out. She held the letter over the flame until it caught and then she dropped the paper into the sink. She watched it burn for a minute, then turned a knob beside a metal tube that curved over the basin of the sink. Water came out of the tube.

"Have you thought about what name you are going to go by?" she asked Eirian, turning the knob to make the water stop.

Eirian shook her head. "Not really. We did not have much time to prepare."

"Hmm, what about Elaine?" suggested Charity.

"It seems as good a name as any," said Eirian.

"This is the name you will be going by for however long you will be here, as good a name as any' is not good enough." Charity disappeared into one of the bedrooms and reappeared carrying a book. "Here, look through this and see if you can find one that you love. Can you read or speak English?"

Eirian nodded. She handed Aubree to Claudette and took the book.

"English, Chinese, and Spanish were all part of my lessons," explained Eirian. "I was required to learn them, in case I needed to come to the Mortal Realm for any reason. I am thankful for those lessons, now."

Charity chuckled. "Good."

"From this point on, I think we should switch to English," said Claudette in English. "We do not want our language to give us away. Most mortals would not think anything of it, but other fae would certainly recognize Elvish. We need to blend in as much as possible."

Eirian sat on the couch and flipped through the pages of the name book. She considered each name, mentally trying them on. She smiled as her eyes fell on a particular name.

"Ariana," she said, remembering to speak English at the last moment. "I like the name Ariana."

Charity smiled. "Ariana it is, then. Welcome to the Mortal Realm, Ariana."

Charity offered the spare bedroom to Eirian and Aubree and pulled a hidden bed from the couch for Claudette and Marcia. Charity showed Eirian how to use the shower and lent her a pair of pajamas.

Eirian, exhausted, climbed into bed and curled herself around her baby sister, grateful for the day to be over. She dreaded the future. She listened to the sounds of the strange new world she would now call home and wondered how long she would she would have to stay here.

7

Eirian woke up alone. Panic consumed her; Aubree was gone. She threw off the blankets and rushed into the living room. She sighed in relief, calming her pounding heart. Claudette sat on the sofa, nursing Aubree.

"Good, you are awake," smiled Claudette, looking up from the baby. "I thought I would let you sleep in. You have had a rough day."

"More like a rough several months," yawned Eirian.

She sat down beside Claudette. Aubree latched off Claudette's breast and smiled up at her sister.

"Here," Claudette handed Aubree to Eirian. "I think she is finished for now."

"Where is Charity?" asked Eirian.

"She went out to buy clothes and such for us," Claudette replied, heading into the kitchen. "She should be back soon. Are you hungry?"

Eirian nodded. "What do I do now?" she asked.

"Nothing today. Right now, all you need to do is try to relax. In a few days we will begin looking for a place of our own. Eventually we will need to get jobs, so we can survive on our own instead of relying on Charity." She chuckled at the unintended joke. She returned carrying a plate with bread and honey, with slices of apple on top, and a glass of milk. She set it all down on the short table in front of them and held out her hands for the baby.

"Just a word of warning," she said, as Eirian picked up the plate. "The food here takes some getting used to."

Eirian took a bite and discovered what Claudette meant. The food tasted bland compared to the food at home. The bread had a strange texture, the honey not quite as sweet, and the apples were slightly bitter. Even the milk tasted different. Eirian finished breakfast and carried her plate to the kitchen, when Charity returned.

"I picked up a stray wandering around outside," joked Charity, entering the apartment, arms loaded with bags.

Eirian curiously looked at the door as a man followed Charity inside.

"Elior!" Eirian jumped off the couch and threw her arms around his neck.

The change in Elior was not nearly as drastic as it was in Eirian. He was already half-human, and the glamour simply enhanced his humanity. His blue eyes were not as bright as they once were, his hair darker and yellow. She found him no less handsome. Elior dropped the bags he carried and pulled Eirian close. She kissed him without any thought about the other women in the room. They broke apart and Eirian blushed, realizing what she did. She turned around to see Charity and Claudette grinning.

"You—you will not tell my parents about this, will you?" asked Eirian.

Claudette laughed. "Dear, I have known the both of you since the day you were born. I have long suspected that you two felt more strongly about each other than you let on."

"Does that mean that my parents—" began Eirian.

"No, I do not think they suspect anything," answered Claudette, anticipating Eirian's question.

Eirian sighed in relief. She wanted to talk to Elior, to ask him why he was there, but Charity made him help her carry in the rest of her shopping. He finally sat down beside Eirian on the sofa.

"How did you get here?" asked Eirian.

"Your father sent me. He went to find me shortly after you left, which wasn't hard. I was spying on you," admitted Elior. "When I heard you coming back to the courtyard, I hid. I saw everything. Anyway, your father went to find me. He said that the thought of you and Aubree being here alone, even with Claudette and Charity watching over you, was too much for him. He wanted someone he could trust, someone you trusted, to help protect you."

"He really sent you after us?" asked Eirian. Elior nodded and Eirian leaned into him. "I am glad. To be honest, the thought of being away from you was more unbearable than the thought of being away from them. Does that make me a bad daughter?" Eirian looked up at Claudette.

"No, Dear." Claudette shook her head. "It does not make you a bad daughter. It only means that you truly love Elior."

"Speaking of which." Charity picked up the name book. "He probably needs a new name too. 'Elior' is not really a common name in these parts."

Elior raised an eyebrow in confusion when Charity handed him the name book.

"My name is now Ariana." Eirian gave Elior a playful smile.

Elior smiled back. "I love it." He kissed her before opening the book. "What do you think about Elliot?" he asked a few minutes later.

"Ariana and Elliot." Eirian tried the names out. "It has a nice ring to it."

"Good," said Elior. "Then I have a question for you, Ariana."

"And what question would that be, Elliot?"

"It is a question I have been wanting to ask you for a very long time, but couldn't because of our situation. Now, I can't think of a reason why I shouldn't." Elior slid off the couch and knelt in front of her. Tears filled Eirian's wide eyes. Elior took her hand. "Eirian-slash-Ariana, will you marry me?"

Eirian hesitated. "What about my parents? They may not be here right now, but we will return home eventually."

"I thought about that," said Elior. "We have tried to come up with a way for us to be together for years. You aren't a princess here, and I'm not your servant. We're just Arianna and Elliot. Two young people in love. What better opportunity will we have? We can worry about how to tell the king and queen when the time comes for us to go home. Besides, wasn't it you who told me it was sometimes better to ask for forgiveness than permission?

"I love you, Eirian. I am willing to take this risk in order to finally, openly, be with you. Are you?"

Eirian nodded. Elior always knew just what to say to alleviate her worries. "Yes. I am willing to take this risk with you, Elior. I love you and I will marry you, here, in the Mortal Realm." She slid off the couch and into his arms.

Elior held her close. "Sorry. I don't have a ring."

Eirian laughed and kissed him.

"Well, at least now we don't have to worry about finding you separate homes," chuckled Charity.

The next several weeks left Eirian very little time to relax. Two days after their arrival, Charity handed Claudette, Eirian, and Elior small cards made out of a material Charity called "plastic." The cards had their new names printed on them along with their pictures. The ease of getting her picture taken surprised Eirian. Mortal devices called "cameras" instantly captured the likeness of their targets. Charity tried to explain how the cameras, and many other things in this world worked, but she used words like "digitally" and "electronically" that went over Eirian's head.

Eirian gradually learned to speak in a less formal manner. Mortal English was similar to the Common language spoken in the Faerie Realm, both stemming from a time when mortals and fae co-existed. Try as she might, Eirian could not entirely rid herself of her Elvish accent. Charity told her not to worry. It took her nearly a century to lose her own accent.

Eirian enjoyed when she, Claudette, and Charity went shopping for a wedding dress and when she and Elior looked at apartments and houses. The thought of finally being able to spend the rest of her life with Elior, without having to hide, made all the other problems feel far away. Whatever challenges arose, they could face them together. When her father called them back home, it would be too late for him to argue; provided he called them after the wedding took place. Eirian felt the subterfuge slightly dishonest, but then Elior held her and kissed her and the feeling passed. Eirian could never see herself with anyone except Elior. Her parents would have to come to terms with their relationship eventually.

The day arrived and they stood in a small church for the ceremony. Claudette, Charity, and some of Charity's neighbors that Eirian knew attended. Marcia was the flower girl. Eirian stood outside the door to the sanctuary of the church. A pang of sadness struck her heart and she wiped away a tear. Her father was not there to give her away. Her mother was not waiting for her on the other side of the door. *We can have another ceremony in front of the whole kingdom when we return.* The thought put a smile on her face.

Eirian heard the music begin and the doors opened. Elior stood at the altar, dressed in a white suit. Charity and Claudette stood on either side of him. Aubree, dressed in her tiny gold dress, filled Claudette's arms. Marcia picked at the flower petals in her basket. Eirian took a step forward, willing her shaking legs to carry her down the aisle. Elior took her hands and strength returned to her body. The minister began, but Eirian hardly heard what he said. Eliot squeezed her hands, reminding her to speak.

"Elliot," she began. "I have loved you for many years, and I promise to love you for many years more. No matter what happens, I promise to stand by your side.

No matter how hard things get or how bad they may appear, anything is possible as long as we are together." She took the ring from Charity and slid it onto Elior's finger. "This ring stands as a promise, from now to the end of time itself, that I belong to you and to you alone."

"Ariana," Elior looked deep into his bride's eyes. "I cannot remember a time when you and I were not together in some way or another, first as playmates, then friends, then more than friends. You have always been there, and I know you always will be. You and I are embarking on a new adventure together, an adventure that many people say is terrifying, but one I am looking forward to. No matter what we may face, I will stand by you, love you, and protect you." He took the ring from Claudette and slid it onto Eirian's finger. "This ring stands as a promise, from now to the end of time itself, that I belong to you and to you alone."

"If there is any here who believe that these two should not be joined in holy matrimony, speak now or forever hold your peace." The minister paused. "Then, with the power vested in me by God, I now pronounce you man and wife. You may kiss the bride."

Eirian and Elior moved into a small, beautiful wooden house near Charity's apartment building. Claudette and Marcia lived with them until Aubree weaned, then moved into an apartment in Charity's building. Neither Aubree nor Marcia knew anything about their true identities, though it pained Eirian to keep the truth a secret. The girls grew up as mortals. Aubree believed Charity and Claudette to be her aunts, and Marcia, her cousin. No one spoke Elvish, or any other Fae language, around the girls.

Eirian never forgot her true heritage. She retained her royal elegance, though she tempered it with human mediocrity. Charity helped Eirian and Elior find jobs; Elior as a groundskeeper at the church where they were married, and Eirian at a flower shop.

Eirian desperately missed her parents. She dreamed about them and struggled, especially early on, to force herself out of bed. Elior – whose mother remined behind in the Faerie Realm – helped keep depression at bay. He daily reminded her of their mission, and she did the same for him. Years passed yet Eirian still heard no word from her parents.

At least Aubree is safe. That is what matters. That is why we are here. Keeping Aubree out of Tola's sights is the only thing that matters.

8

Fifteen years later

"Aubree, this is the third time your alarm has gone off! If you don't wake up now, you're going to be late!" Ariana's voice cut through Aubree's precious dream about the cute waiter from the Moon Drop Café.

"I'm up!" Aubree drowsily shouted back.

She groaned, rolled over, and shut off her alarm. She wanted to close her eyes and re-enter her dream, but knew that Ariana and Elliot would have a cow if she was late for school. Aubree got dressed and went down the hall to the living room. A sea green sofa separated the living and dining rooms. Opposite the sofa, above the mantle, hung a large, flat-screen television. Family portraits decorated the area, from the walls to the mantle, and side tables on either side of the couch. Ariana sat at the round table dining table, her back to a pair of sliding glass doors that opened to her garden, arranging flowers in a crystal vase. Aubree picked her open backpack up off the floor beside the front door, stuffing fallen papers back inside.

"Hey, Ana, have you seen my history book?" Aubree lifted one of the couch cushions. "Never mind, I found it."

"Aubree, I appreciate you doing the laundry, but I don't think this belongs to either Ariana or me." Elliot walked out of his bedroom carrying a purple and white striped blouse.

"Sorry." Aubree took the blouse from Elliot and stuffed it into her backpack.

Ariana shook her head. "Honestly, Aubree, you need to be more careful with your things."

"Sorry," Aubree repeated. She went over to the coffee pot and poured some into her travel mug. "I don't have time for breakfast. I'll just stop by the café on my way to school and pick up a muffin or something."

"I'm sure you will," teased Ariana.

Aubree felt a blush color her cheeks. She spun around and saw a smirk on Ariana's face. "What's that supposed to mean?"

"Nothing, just that you've been spending an awful lot of time at that café lately." Ariana nonchalantly adjusted her flowers.

"Yes, you're there just about every day," added Elliot.

"So?" shrugged Aubree, taking a sip from her mug. "There's nothing wrong with the café."

Please, drop the subject. she silently begged.

"There's nothing wrong with the waiter either." Ariana gave Aubree a playful wink.

Aubree choked on her coffee. Elior pounded Aubree's back to help clear her lungs as she coughed.

"I—I don't know what you're talking about," she stammered. "I go to the café because I like the muffins."

"Whatever you say." Ariana walked over and kissed Aubree on the forehead as someone knocked on the front door. "Have fun at school."

"Yeah, like that's possible," muttered Aubree. She walked over to let Marcia in so they could walk to school together.

"Then have fun after school," teased Elliot.

Aubree's blush deepened and she hurried out the door, pulling it closed behind her.

"What was that about?" Marcia walked beside Aubree down the sidewalk.

Aubree looked at the sky and groaned. "Apparently Ariana and Elliot have seen me in the café."

"Man, that's rough." Marcia sympathetically patted Aubree on the shoulder. "It makes me glad I'm an only child. Does this mean you don't want to stop in for a muffin today?"

"I think it'll be okay." Aubree did not want to miss out on seeing *him* before school. "They already know why I really go, and I didn't eat at home, so..."

"Right, come on." Marcia chuckled. She slipped her arm through Aubree's and steered toward the Moon Drop Café.

Ariana smiled as Aubree left.

"Ah, young love," she sighed.

"Don't you think she's a little young to be in love?" asked Elliot.

"It was just a figure of speech," shrugged Ariana.

"If you say so." Elliot walked over and kissed her. "I've got to go, too. I'll see you this evening."

"Be safe." Ariana returned the kiss. "I love you."

"I love you, too." Elliot walked out the door.

Ariana walked back over to the table to finish arranging the flowers.

Aubree considered going straight home after school to, hopefully, convince her sister and brother-in-law that there was nothing going on between her and the waiter. That was true. Aubree only spoke to the waiter when she ordered something. She spent most of the time pretending to do homework and watching him.

Aubree, lost in thought, let her feet make the decision for her; she stood outside the Moon Drop Café. Through the large, plate glass window bearing the café's logo, she saw him. He stood beside a table, taking the order of a scarred, dark-haired woman, one of the café regulars. He looked up at Aubree. His eyes met hers. A tingle, like electricity, ran down Aubree's spine.

His eyes caught her attention the first time she saw him. They were a strange color; an orange-brown that almost looked yellow at times. She wished he would not hide them behind his shaggy black hair.

Aubree pushed open the door, smiling at the unique wolf howl that accompanied the action, and walked to an empty table. She pulled a textbook out of her backpack and pretended to read. He appeared at her side a moment later.

"Caramel macchiato with extra cinnamon and a chocolate chip muffin?"

"Excuse me?" Aubree looked up.

"That's what you usually order, right?" he asked. "A caramel macchiato with extra cinnamon and a chocolate chip muffin?"

"Oh, right." Aubree chuckled in embarrassment. "Yes, please."

He turned to walk away, stopped, and turned back to her. "My name's Reima, by the way."

"I know," said Aubree. Reima raised an eyebrow. "Umm, I—I mean, it's on your name tag." Aubree nervously nodded at the plastic pin on the front of Reima's uniform. "M—my name's Aubree."

"Nice to meet you, Aubree," smiled Reima. "Officially, I mean."

Aubree awkwardly nodded in response.

"Well, I should go put your order in." Reima gestured at the counter behind him.

Aubree nodded again and Reima walked away.

Aubree smacked herself in the head. "'I know?'" she muttered. "Great, now he's going to think you're a stalker or a weirdo or something." She groaned and dropped her head onto the table. Ariana always said that first impressions can often make or break a relationship. If true, then Aubree felt certain she blew any chance of a relationship with Reima.

Reima came back a few minutes later with Aubree's order.

"You must really like here, huh?" he asked. "You've come just about every day for the past few months."

"Have I?" Aubree tried to sound nonchalant. "I haven't noticed. I just—I like your muffins—the café's muffins. You make good muffins," she sheepishly added.

"I'm sure Teegan will be glad to hear that," laughed Reima. "She is very proud of her muffins."

Aubree chuckled.

"Well, I should really get back to work," said Reima. "Let me know if there's anything else you need. It was nice officially meeting you."

Aubree tucked a strand of blond hair behind her ear. "Same here."

Reima smiled and went back to his other customers. Aubree took her time eating her muffin, dragging out her time at the café for as long as possible.

She finished eating, stuffed her textbook back into her bag, and went to pay her bill. She delightfully smiled when Reima came to the register.

"Did you enjoy everything?" he asked as he told Aubree her total.

Aubree nodded, handing him a $20 bill. "Thank you."

"Thank *you*," said Reima. "I'll see you tomorrow?"

Aubree frowned in confusion. "I don't have school tomorrow."

"I know." Reima brushed the hair out of his eyes only to have it fall back into place. "I was hoping you'd stop by anyway."

"Oh! Um, okay." Aubree nodded. "I think I can stop by."

"Then it's a date." Reima handed Aubree her change and receipt. "I'll see you at noon."

"Okay. See you then."

Reima smiled and went back to work. Aubree dropped her change into the tip jar and walked out the door.

Did he just say date? thought Aubree. *More importantly, did I just agree?* She fought to contain herself until she got home.

"Ariana?" Aubree called through the front door. "Elliot? Is anyone home?" She listened for a response but heard none. A smile split her face and she let out a squeal, dancing in place. She spun in a circle and abruptly stopped when she spotted her sister, unsuccessfully trying to hide a smile, standing in the kitchen.

"Something exciting happen at school today?" asked Ariana.

Aubree blushed. "H—how much of that did you see?"

"Enough to wish I had my camera out," chuckled Ariana.

"I thought you weren't home." Aubree scratched the back of her head in embarrassment.

"I was out in the garden," Ariana nodded towards the back door. "I came in when I heard you call and, well, you know the rest."

"Please don't tell Elliot about this," begged Aubree. "He'll tease me."

"You tell me what's gotten you excited like that, and I'll consider it," said Ariana.

"Ana," pleaded Aubree.

Ariana shrugged her shoulders, a grin on her face.

"That's the dea–" Ariana stopped mid-word, her grin fading away. She put a hand to her chest and closed her eyes

"Ariana?" Aubree took a step closer to her sister. "Are you okay?"

The woman nodded. "I'm fine."

"What just happened? Are you okay?"

"I'm fine," Ariana assured her. She took a deep breath and opened her eyes. "It was just a flash of a very painful memory."

"Like about what happened to Mom and Dad?"

"Something like that." Ariana smiled, but it did not quite reach her eyes. "I need to get back to the garden. I want to be finished in time to make dinner before Elliot gets home. Why don't you get started on your homework?"

Ariana walked out the back door without waiting for a response. Aubree stared after her. Ariana often had flashes of memory and Aubree never knew what triggered them. Sometimes it was the simplest things, like a walk through the park. One time, Aubree found a cool arrowhead made out of a shiny black stone, and Ariana completely freaked out. Aubree did not know how her parents died. No one ever spoke about it, and Aubree was too afraid to ask. If simple things caused Ariana to have such a strong reaction, Aubree could only imagine what those questions would do.

Ariana did not notice when Elliot got home. She stood in the middle of the kitchen, staring absently at the oven. She jumped when she felt his arms wrap around her from behind.

"Hey, it's just me," Elliot gently spoke into Ariana's ear.

Ariana sighed and relaxed into his embrace. "I'm sorry."

"Is everything okay?" asked Elliot. "Did something happen today?"

"I think I worried Aubree. We were talking and I—I almost said the word 'deal' and then I froze, because, all of a sudden, I heard *her* voice, and I just—I couldn't—" Tears filled Ariana's eyes.

Elliot turned her around to face him and held her close. "Shhh." He tenderly caressed her hair. "It's alright. She doesn't know where we live. Aubree's safe. It'll be okay."

The oven timer went off. Ariana pulled back and wiped her eyes.

"Aubree! Can you come set the table?" she called, pulling the chicken casserole out of the oven and carrying it to the table.

Aubree came out of her room. She placed the plates and silverware around the table. "Hey, can I go out tomorrow?" she asked.

"Go out with whom?" asked Elliot.

Aubree glanced at Ariana. She raised her eyebrows, eyes wide, in a pleading expression, silently begging Ariana not to mention what had happened earlier that day. Ariana calmly took another bite of her supper, giving nothing away.

"Just a friend," answered Aubree.

"Which friend would that be?" asked Ariana, a half smile on her face.

"Just—a friend," Aubree noncommittally repeated.

"Not Marcia," guessed Elliot.

Aubree shook her head. "A different friend. Besides, Marcia's not a friend, she's my cousin."

"Better not let her hear you say that." Elliot sipped his water.

"What, exactly, would you and this 'different friend' be doing?" asked Ariana.

Aubree shrugged. "We're just going to hang out."

"So, you want to go hang out with a friend." Ariana emphasized the last word with a nod. "Would I be wasting my time if I asked you to clarify?"

Aubree gave her a pleading look, which Ariana met with raised eyebrows. Aubree sighed.

"It's the waiter from Moon Drop," she admitted. "He asked me to stop by tomorrow."

"Ah, the truth comes out," said Elliot.

"Can I go?" asked Aubree.

"Are you asking for permission, or asking if you are physically capable of going?" asked Ariana.

"*May* I go?" Aubree amended with a roll of her eyes.

Ariana and Elliot looked at each other. "What do you think?" asked Elliot.

Ariana made a show of considering the offer. "I don't see why not," a hopeful grin spread across Aubree's face, "but you have to finish your homework and help with the dishes."

Aubree excitedly nodded her head. "Promise!"

Ariana and Elliot smiled.

"And I want you to call if things start to get out of hand," added Elliot.

Aubree nodded again. "Thank you!"

"She acts like she expected us to say no." Elliot looked at Ariana.

"It's like she doesn't know us at all." Ariana playfully pouted. "Now that that's out of the way. How was school today?"

Hidden Identity

9

Aubree woke up the next morning well before time for her to leave. She looked through her closet for the right outfit to wear. Her first choice was an orange sun dress she bought the previous week at the mall with Marcia, but it made her look twelve. Jeans and a T-shirt looked too casual. She finally settled on a baby blue blouse and black skirt. Aubree braided her hair, like always, and wished she had some blush, or even a little lipstick, to make her look less pale. Even though she would be sixteen in a few months, Ariana still would not let her wear makeup.

Aubree finished getting ready and went into the living room where Ariana and Elliot sat together on the sofa. They looked up when she entered.

"How do I look?" Aubree twirled in place.

Ariana smiled. "You look very lovely."

Aubree's eyes filled with hope. "Really?"

Ariana nodded. "Your first date. I can't believe you're old enough for that already. I only wish—" tears filled her eyes and she shook her head.

Aubree touched her sister's arm. "I know." Ariana did not like talking about their parents. "I wish they were here, too."

Ariana smiled through her tears and got up to hug Aubree, careful not to mess up her outfit.

"I don't know if I would call this an actual date, anyway." Aubree pulled back. "All he said was that he wanted me to stop by the café."

Elliot chuckled. "I saw the way he looked at you when I passed by a couple days ago. Trust me, it's a date."

"Yeah, but if I think about it like a date and something goes wrong—"

"Nothing will go wrong." Ariana dried her eyes with the back of her index fingers. "You'll be fine."

"But what if we start talking and we find out we have nothing in common?" Aubree toyed with the edge of her blouse.

"Then you try to find something you do have in common," said Elliot. "Or you shake hands and part ways."

"I don't want to shake hands and part ways."

Ariana took Aubree's hands. "Just be yourself and see what happens. You never know until you try."

"As always, your use of clichéd platitudes is completely correct," laughed Elliot.

Aubree smiled. "Okay, I'm off."

"Have fun, but not too much fun," winked Elliot, earning him a smack on the arm from Ariana.

"Remember, call if you need us and be home before dinner," Ariana said to Aubree.

Aubree smiled and agreed as she walked out the door. Her phone buzzed, when she passed Aunt Claudette's apartment building; a text from Marcia.

I want to hear all the details when you get back.

Smiling, Aubree looked up to see her cousin standing in the window. Aubree waved to her, and Marcia gave her a thumbs up.

Will do. Aubree typed in reply.

Aubree arrived at the café and found the owner, Teegan, waiting for her. Teegan was a tall, muscular woman with short, spiked black hair, bright red lipstick, and thick eyeliner around her green eyes. A dragon tattoo coiled around her neck and down her left shoulder. Aubree found Teegan's appearance too intimidating to ever try talking to her.

"You must be Aubree." Teegan held out a hand for Aubree to shake. "I'm Teegan. Reima is upstairs. He'll be down in a minute."

Aubree gave Teegan a nervous smile and shook her hand. Teegan's grip was stronger than Aubree expected.

"Listen," Teegan put an arm around Aubree's shoulder. "I know Reima may seem dark and mysterious, but he can be really sensitive at times. Don't do anything to hurt him, 'kay?"

"Why would I hurt him?" asked Aubree.

"I'm just saying."

"Teegan, please don't scare Aubree off before I even get a chance to talk to her." Reima walked through the open café to them. He smiled at Aubree. "You look beautiful."

Reima wore a plain, navy T-shirt and dark blue jeans. Aubree blushed and self-consciously toyed with the tip of her braid.

Did I overdress? she thought.

"I'm not scaring her. We were just introducing ourselves. Isn't that right, Aubree?" Teegan squeezed Aubree's shoulder.

Aubree winced. She assumed the action was meant to be friendly, but it still hurt. "Right." She gave Reima a weak smile.

Teegan took her arm off Aubree's shoulder. "Well, I have to get back to the customers. You two have fun. Remember, your shift starts at three." Teegan pointed at Reima. "You'd better not leave me running this place on my own all day."

Reima rolled his eyes. "I know my schedule. It's not like this is my first day."

"No, but it is your first date." Teegan winked. "I just don't want you to lose track of time." Teegan started to turn away, but stopped and looked at Reima, all trace of playfulness gone. "Be careful."

Reima looked Teegan in the eye and nodded.

"Goodbye, Teegan." Reima held open the door for Aubree. "Sorry about her." He led Aubree down the sidewalk, away from the café. "She can be a bit much."

Aubree quickly shook her head. "No, she seems nice."

"She's friendly enough most of the time," Reima agreed, "but you really don't want to see her when she's angry."

"She must not be that bad if you choose to keep working for her."

"*With* her, actually," said Reima. "She may not act like it, but I own just as much of the café as she does."

"Really? Cool." *How old is he?* "Um, where are we going?"

Reima nodded down the sidewalk. "To the park. I thought a picnic brunch thing where we could just sit and talk would be nice. Get to know each other a little, you know?"

"But you don't have a picnic basket."

"It's already there, I went early to find a spot."

"Oh."

Westin Park bustled with people taking advantage of the last few weeks of warmth before fall. Joggers circled the gravel path with their dogs, children played tag beside a large lake, couples sat together on wooden benches.

Reima led Aubree to a spot under a large oak tree. He had a blanket spread out on the ground with a picnic basket in the middle. Marvin, the Willow-man he asked to watch his spot, sat under the tree.

"Thanks for keeping an eye on this stuff for me," Reima said to him.

Marvin nodded his head and silently walked away. Reima knelt down on the blanket and unloaded the basket.

"Who was that?" asked Aubree.

"A friend of mine. I asked him to make sure no one took our spot, or my basket." Reima patted the ground next to him. "Sit down."

"I picked the perfect day to wear a skirt," muttered Aubree. She sat down on the blanket with her legs off to the side, mermaid style.

"Tell me about yourself." Reima opened the basket.

"Um, well, I live with my sister and her husband," began Aubree. "My parents died when I was a baby, and we lived with my aunt until I was about three."

Reima sympathetically nodded. "I'm sorry to hear that. I haven't seen my parents in a long time."

"What happened to them?"

"Nothing, as far as I know. My dad and I got into a big fight and he kicked me out."

"I'm sorry."

Reima shrugged, ignoring the pain that still felt fresh, even after all this time. "It was a long time ago." He wanted to keep the focus of the conversation on Aubree. "Then, it's just you, your sister, and her husband?"

"Pretty much. Like I said we lived with my aunt for a while and she has a daughter, Marcia, who's like another sister and we have another aunt who lives close by, but that's it."

"Sounds nice. Are you all pretty close?"

Aubree nodded, and Reima felt a small pang of jealousy.

"What about you?" asked Aubree. "Any brothers or sisters?"

Reima chuckled. "I have eleven siblings."

"Eleven?" Aubree's eyes widened in shock.

"Yeah, one older brother, three older sisters, three younger sisters and four younger brothers."

"Wow. Are you close to any of them?" asked Aubree.

"Some of them," Reima answered. "But I haven't heard from them since I left home."

"Why not?"

"It's complicated." He shifted uncomfortably. He did not like to talk about his past, especially with mortals.

Aubree gently touched his arm. "It's okay. You don't have to tell me if you don't want to."

"Thank you," he smiled at her.

He chided himself, *Be careful. She's mortal. It's dangerous to get attached to mortals, especially for a Wolf. You know what will happen if you fall in love with her.*

Reima felt himself developing feelings for this mortal girl from the moment she walked into the café. He asked her out in the hopes that reality would not be able to compare to his expectations and that his feelings toward her would fade away into feelings of friendship. Though nothing compared to a romantic relationship, friendship with a mortal was still dangerous.

"Tell me more about yourself, what do you like to do, what's your favorite color?" If they stayed on superficial topics like that, there was less chance of a deeper relationship forming.

Aubree laughed when she saw Reima packed muffins for their picnic meal as a nod back to their first official meeting. They ate and spoke about their interests until it was almost time for Reima to get back to work.

"So, uh, Reima?" Aubree asked as they walked back to the café. "Can I ask you a question?"

"Isn't that what we've been doing all day?" he replied. "Go ahead."

"Um, how – how old are you?" she asked. "Because you're not in school, you own a business, and you say it's been a long time since you've seen your family, but you don't look old enough to have all of that happen yet."

The age question, Reima hated the age question. He did not like lying, but there was no way he could tell her the truth.

He gave her his standard answer. "I'm twenty. I was home schooled, and I graduated early."

"Oh." Aubree sounded disappointed.

"Is a bad thing?" he asked.

"I'm only fifteen," she responded, "but I'll be sixteen in a couple months. I don't want my age to scare you off."

Reima laughed out loud. *She's worried about scaring* me *off? If she only knew.* He cleared his throat at the confused look on her face.

"You won't scare me off," he promised. "We just met. I think it only best if we start out as friends, anyway." *And then stay that way.* He added to himself.

"That sounds good," she sighed in relief.

They reached the café. Reima waved at Teegan through the glass to let her know he was there.

Aubree shyly rubbed her arm. "I guess I'll see you on Monday, after school?"

Reima smiled. "Definitely. I'm glad you could come today."

"Me, too." Aubree glanced up at him. She bit her bottom lip. "I know we're just supposed to be friends right now, but would it be okay if I hugged you?"

Reima chuckled. "Friends can't hug each other?" He nodded. "I think a hug will be okay."

She hugged him and he hugged her back, the scent of her shampoo reaching his nose. *Maybe a hug wasn't such a good idea.*

"Well, see you later." Aubree let go and walked down the street.

"See you." Reima waved after her.

He walked into the café and went upstairs to the apartment he and Teegan lived in. He smelled Teegan before he heard her. The various smells from the café may have masked her distinctive scent of sulfur from everyone else, but not from Reima's sensitive nose.

"How was your first date?" asked Teegan.

Reima closed his bedroom door and locked it in order to change into his work clothes without Teegan barging in on him.

"It wasn't a date," he answered through the closed door. "I just took her out on a picnic to get to know her."

"Sounds like a date to me," said Teegan. "So, how was it?"

"It was fine."

"Just fine?" Teegan sounded disappointed.

Reima shrugged. "I had a nice time. We talked, we ate, what more do you want?"

"What did you talk about?"

"We talked about what we like and what we don't like. You know, things people normally talk about when they first meet." He tied on his apron and looked around for his order pad.

"Is that all?" asked Teegan.

Reima sighed and opened the door.

"What do you want to hear, Teegan?" he asked. "That she was really nice and beautiful and that I really like her and can't wait to see her again? Because it's true. But I can't feel that way because she's mortal and I'm—" He fell silent.

Teegan put an arm around his shoulder. "I know. I do know what it's like to fall for a mortal. That's why I'm asking. I don't want you to get hurt."

Reima shrugged off Teegan's arm and walked to the corner where the dog slept. Rylee looked up at Reima's approach and wagged her tail. Her stomach bulged with a litter of puppies due any day. He scratched her behind the ear.

"I don't want that either," he said, finally breaking the silence. "That's why I'm trying to make myself see her as just a friend."

"And asking her out on a date is the way to do that?" asked Teegan.

"It wasn't a date!" exclaimed Reima.

Teegan shook her head. "She didn't see it that way, and you did call it a date when you asked her out."

"What was I supposed to do?" asked Reima. "Just ignore her? Pretend I didn't notice every time she walked through the door?"

"You've had plenty of regulars come into the café."

"None like her." Reima gave Rylee a treat and walked downstairs.

He needed to not think about Aubree anymore. If he could make himself see her as just a friend, then maybe he would be okay. Come Monday, he would be sure not to flirt with her. His conversations with her would not go beyond the surface. Eventually, hopefully, he would stop feeling this way.

IO

Giddy from her date, Aubree sent a text to Ariana and Elliot.

I'm going to stop by Marcia's for a while. I'll be home before supper.

A smile plastered itself to Aubree's face. She skipped down the sidewalk to Marcia's apartment building and pushed the intercom button beside Aunt Claudette's name.

"It's open." Marcia's voice crackled from the speaker and she buzzed Aubree in.

Aubree took the elevator up to the sixth floor and found her grinning cousin waiting in the doorway. Marcia giggled at Aubree and pulled her inside the apartment.

"Hello, Aubree," Aunt Claudette called from the living room as the girls passed.

Aubree only had time to wave as Marcia dragged her to her bedroom and closed the door.

"I want to hear everything." Marcia flopped onto her bed. "Don't leave out a single detail."

"Well, first off, he's twenty." Aubree took a seat in Marcia's blue butterfly chair, "so we can't actually start dating until after my birthday."

"Oh? Well, maybe I can have him until then," joked Marcia.

Aubree tossed a pillow that Marcia dodged.

"Keep going," urged Marcia. "Where did you go? What did you do?"

"He took me to the park," said Aubree. "We had a picnic brunch of muffins."

"That's so sweet!" squealed Marcia.

Aubree grinned. "He's really sweet. He's smart, too. He graduated high school early, and, did you know that he is the co-owner of Moon Drop?"

"Really? I thought that lady owned it."

"They both own it."

"Do you think she'll be any competition for you?" asked Marcia.

Aubree shook her head. "I don't think so. They're just friends, and have been for a long time. If there was anything going on between them, he wouldn't have asked me out."

"You never know, some guys are jerks like that."

"Well, Reima's not a jerk," insisted Aubree. "A jerk wouldn't have agreed to just being friends for two months. A jerk would have tried to talk me into dating him without telling anyone."

"A jerk wouldn't have taken you on a picnic for the first date," Marcia pointed out.

"Exactly!"

"Go on, tell me more." Marcia laid down on her stomach and propped her chin up with her hands, ready to listen to all the juicy details.

Aubree recounted the entire date to Marcia, who giggled and squealed at all the correct places.

Aunt Claudette knocked on the door interrupting the girls. "Aubree, Ariana just called. She said you need to get home for dinner and asked why you didn't answer your phone."

Aubree looked at her phone and saw three missed calls and a text from both Ariana and Elliot.

"I have to go." She stood and hugged Marcia goodbye.

Marica put both hands on Aubree's shoulders. She locked eyes with her cousin. "Keep me updated. I want to hear about every single conversation you have with this guy."

"You really need a boyfriend," laughed Aubree.

"You could ask Reima if he has a friend," suggested Marcia.

Aubree laughed again. "I'll see what I can do."

Ariana looked up from setting the table as Aubree came through the door.

"Sorry, I'm late," said Aubree. "I accidently had my phone on silent. Marcia and I were talking, and I lost track of time. I'm sorry."

"It's okay." Ariana kissed Aubree on the top of her head. "Elliot and I set the table. You go on and wash up, and then we can eat."

Ariana waited until they were all at the table to ask about the date. Aubree immediately blushed. She told them all about the picnic.

"Sounds like you enjoyed yourself," said Elliot. "Are you going to see him again?"

Aubree hesitated. "Well, I want to, but he's twenty years old. I'll need your permission."

Elliot choked on his drink. Ariana pounded him on the back.

"Twenty?" Elliot asked when he could speak.

"Yeah, but that's not that big a difference," shrugged Aubree. "I mean, I'll be sixteen in a couple of months. Really it's less than five years."

"That's still a big difference," said Elliot.

"Well, how far apart are you two?" challenged Aubree, though she knew it could not be too large a gap.

Ariana raised her eyebrows. "Elliot is only two years older than me."

Aubree shrank back in her chair.

Ariana saw the disappointed look on her sister's face and softened her expression. "Elliot and I will discuss this later."

Aubree hopefully looked at her sister. "You'll think about it?"

Ariana nodded.

"But nothing's going to happen until you are officially sixteen," Elliot added.

"Thank you," said Aubree.

"Don't thank us yet," warned Ariana. "There's still a chance we'll say no."

They ate dinner and Aubree tried her hardest to make her case by inserting small comments about Reima into the conversation.

After Aubree had gone to bed, Ariana and Elliot sat down on the sofa to talk.

"You're not really thinking about letting her date this guy, are you?" asked Elliot.

"From what Aubree told us, he seems like a good person. Granted, she's only spoken to him twice." Ariana glanced down the hall to make sure Aubree was not eavesdropping, and switched to Elvish, a language they only spoke when they were alone. "Besides, since when is age a problem? Your father was several hundred years younger than your mother."

"True," agreed Elliot in kind. "But this is different."

"We're not talking about them getting married, Elliot, she just wants to spend time with him."

"Yes, I am fully aware of how he wants to spend that time with her," Elliot raised both eyebrows.

Ariana pursed her lips in displeasure. "You can't assume that. How about we meet him, first? We agree they cannot start dating until after her birthday, but what if we tell her that we want to talk to him before then. We can establish rules and boundaries, and, if he ever breaks them, then we cut off the relationship. I don't want her to think she has to go behind our back to see him. We both know firsthand how difficult that makes things."

"You're right. We'll talk to him first," said Elliot.

"Good." Ariana kissed him. "Now, let's go to bed."

Ariana made Aubree wait until Elliot got home from work the next day before she agreed to tell Aubree if they made a decision about Reima.

"If you had gotten up earlier, then we could have discussed it before he left this morning," Ariana calmly told Aubree after the fourth time she asked.

Aubree groaned sat down on the living room couch. She picked up a video game controller and tried to focus on the game on screen.

Why can't Ana just tell me? thought Aubree. *I even cleaned the living room for them!*

She angrily punched the buttons on her controller. The game character fired an arrow, missing the target by a large margin. Aubree sighed and shut off the game. She glanced at the clock.

Elliot should be home any second now.

She turned at the rattle of a key in the lock. The front door opened and Elliot walked in.

"Good! You're home!" Aubree left her controller abandoned on the couch and bounced over to her brother-in-law. She excitedly grabbed him by the arm. "Talk to me."

"Talk to you? About what?" Elliot raised an eyebrow in mock confusion.

"Elliot," whined Aubree.

"Oh! Right, that." Elliot pulled his arm from her grasp. "Let me get in first."

Aubree impatiently tapped her foot while Elliot took off his work boots.

"Aubree, if you are going to act like a child, then the answer is definitely going to be 'no'," scolded Ariana.

"Sorry," muttered Aubree.

She moved her controller to the coffee table and sat down. Her leg bounced while she waited for Elliot and Ariana to join her.

Why do I feel so restless? I only had one real conversation with Reima. A blush creeped into her cheeks. *I mean, he's gorgeous, but what do I really know about him?* She closed her eyes. An image of Reima's orange/brown eyes flashed in her mind and a shiver ran up her spine. Aubree did not believe in love at first sight, not really, that kind of thing only happens in fairy tales. *Then how do I explain what I feel every time I think about him?*

Elliot and Ariana came into the living room. Aubree stopped herself from speaking first and expectantly watched them.

"Before we say anything, we want you to know that we're proud of you for being honest about this," Elliot sat down on the couch. "I know it was hard."

Aubree nodded.

Ariana took Aubree's hands. "You are not a child anymore, and we trust your judgment. Therefore, we have decided to let you continue to spend time with Reima—"

Aubree squeaked in happiness.

"—provided Elliot and I meet him before things go any further."

Aubree nodded her head.

"That's fair," she agreed, a huge grin plastered on her face. She jumped up and hugged her sister and brother-in-law. "Thank you so much!"

Ariana and Elliot smiled and hugged her back.

Reima busily refilled the sugar canisters at the pastry counter. He kept an eye on the customers, ready to help should anyone signal him. Teegan walked up to the counter.

"You see that guy in the corner?" she nodded to a man at a corner table. He sat stock still, staring at the door.

"Yeah, I've asked him three times if I could take his order, and he just glared at me," said Reima. "I nearly growled at him after the third time."

Teegan shook her head. "I don't like the feeling he gives me."

"Do you want me to get rid of him?"

"Nah, I'll do it. You've got company." Teegan nodded to the door where Aubree and another blonde-haired girl entered. Teegan winked at him, and then walked over to the man in the corner.

Reima waved at Aubree and pointed to a table; two cups of coffee and a couple of muffins waited for her. Aubree and her friend went over to the table.

Reima finished his current project and hurried over to join them. "Hey, sorry, I didn't know you were bringing a friend. Let me go get her something really quick."

Aubree shook her head. "That's okay. She's not staying. She just wanted to meet you."

"Marcia." The girl stuck out a hand in greeting. "I'm Aubree's cousin."

"Reima." Reima shook her hand. "It's nice to meet you."

"It sure is." Marcia winked at Reima. Aubree smacked her on the arm.

"What?" Marcia innocently batted her eyelashes at Aubree. "Did I do something wrong?"

Aubree rolled her eyes, but smiled.

Marcia laughed. "Fine, I'll leave you two alone." She picked up one of the muffins, took a bite, and put it back down on the plate before skipping across the café and out the door. She continued to skip down the sidewalk, but stopped outside the window, blew a kiss in their direction, and went on her way. Aubree sat down after her cousin disappeared from sight.

Aubree awkwardly chuckled. "So, yeah, that was my cousin. She just *really* wanted to meet you."

"Am I really that interesting?" chuckled Reima

"I think you are." Aubree shyly smiled.

Reima stopped laughing. *Change the topic. Don't let her ask about you.* "I'm really not that interesting. I live and work at this café. That's pretty much all there is to know." *That I am able to tell you about.*

"I don't believe that." She put her hand over his. He glanced down and she followed his gaze. She quickly pulled her hand back, her eyes wide. "Sorry," she muttered.

"It's okay." Reima heard Rylee moving upstairs. "Hey, do you like dogs?"

Aubree gave an excited nod. "They're my favorite animal. I keep asking Ariana for a puppy, but she just keeps saying she'll think about it. Do you have a dog?"

Reima tilted his head side to side. "Sort of. I don't actually own Rylee, I just feed her and let her stay in the apartment when it's cold. She's upstairs right now because she's pregnant."

Aubree's eyes lit up. "Can I go see her? Or is that inappropriate since we've only just met?"

Reima smiled. "I think it's okay. We're just going to see the dog, and she's in the living room." He stood and held out his hand to help her up.

Aubree followed Reima to a flight of stairs in the back of the café that led to his apartment.

"You really live here, above the café?" she asked.

"Yeah," said Reima. "Teegan and I live here together. It's much easier that way. There's absolutely no commute."

Reima chuckled and Aubree forced herself to laugh around a sudden pang of jealousy.

Aubree stopped in the doorway of the sparsely decorated apartment. She saw no pictures; none of Reima, Teegan, or their families. A large oil painting of a black dragon, sitting on the edge of a cliff, adorned the wall beside the door. The dragon spread its wings; its mouth open in a roar Aubree swore she heard echo in her mind. The smooth, wooden furniture appeared handmade – from the frame to the cushions on the sofa and chairs. A single, rustic-looking rug sat in the center of the living room. A paneled kitchen bar separated the living room from a small kitchen on the opposite side of the apartment. A rough, dark wood table with two matching chairs sat in a small corner near the kitchen, beside a door leading outside. A darkened hallway ran toward the left, leading to other rooms. The entire apartment appeared to have polished, hardwood floors.

"Rylee's over here." Reima walked over to a corner of the living room, between the kitchen bar and a brick fireplace, where a very pregnant border collie rested on a makeshift bed of blankets.

She wagged her tail at their approach. Reima knelt down and scratched Rylee behind the ears.

Aubree knelt down beside him and held out her hand for Rylee to sniff. "Hi, Rylee. You're such a pretty girl."

Rylee sniffed Aubree's hand and then bowed her head, giving Aubree permission to pet her.

"She's really soft."

Reima smiled. "She's a sweetheart, that's for sure."

"When do you think the puppies will come?" asked Aubree.

"Any day now, I should think."

"Can you call me when they do?" Rylee laid her head down on Aubree's knee and looked up at Reima, as if reading and echoing Aubree's thoughts.

"I think I can do that," said Reima. "I'll, um—I'll need your phone number, though."

Aubree blushed.

"Right." She took a notebook out of her backpack and wrote down her cell number. "Here." She tore out the part with her number and handed it to him. Reima took her notebook and wrote his number down.

"So you'll know it's me." He looked up and his eyes locked on hers. Those strange, beautiful eyes.

Reima cleared his throat and looked away.

"I—I should go," said Aubree. "I've got homework."

"Yeah." Reima folded the piece of paper with her number and put it in his pocket. Aubree could not wait until her sixteenth birthday.

Reima walked Aubree back downstairs to the café. He hugged her goodbye and watched her walk down the sidewalk. She turned back to wave. He waved back with a grin. His other hand went to his pocket with her phone number inside. His fingers closed around the slip of paper.

So much for trying to think of her as just a friend. He remembered the way his heart raced when they locked eyes. He sighed and turned back to the customers. Teegan intercepted him before he took two steps. She gripped his arm, digging sharp fingernails into the soft skin of his forearm.

"Ow! Teegan, you're hurting me." Reima tried to pull his arm free, but Teegan held on tighter.

She dragged him to the back room and locked the door. She turned to him, her face white as a sheet. Reima's stomach dropped to his toes. Few things frightened a dragon.

"You remember that guy that was in here earlier?" whispered Teegan.

"Yeah?" replied Reima. "What about him?"

"He's a spy," said Teegan. "For Tola."

Reima's blood ran cold.

"Are you sure?" he asked. "How do you know?"

Teegan nervously chewed on her bottom lip.

"I made a deal with her once, a long time ago," she admitted. "It was a stupid thing, I know, but I was young, barley a hatchling."

Reima nodded in understanding, encouraging her to go on. Teegan was the first person to find Reima after his banishment to the Mortal Realm. She took care of him, showed him how to live in this world. He trusted her.

"I didn't recognize this guy at first, because of his human glamour," Teegan continued, "but the harder I looked, it hit me."

"What does Tola want in this world?" asked Reima.

"Who knows?" responded Teegan, throwing up her hands. "She's probably after someone who didn't hold up their end of a deal and came here to hide."

"Why was her spy here at the café?"

"It's a café owned by two exiled faeries," Teegan pointed out. "Where else would you look?"

"Good point. We'll be okay, though. Tola can't do anything on this side of the Veil," said Reima. "All her powers will be trapped under her human glamour."

Teegan did not answer.

"Right?" prompted Reima, worried by Teegan's silence. "She won't be able to do anything here, so we don't have any reason to worry."

"I need to go." Teegan pushed past Reima. She passed through the back room and exited the café.

Reima tried to focus on work, but his thoughts strayed to Teegan and her strange behavior. The Veil acted as a barrier, not just separating the two worlds, but separating fae from their magic. The Veil covered fae in a strong glamour, making them appear human and hiding almost everything that made them faerie.

Teegan's response gave Reima pause. *Has Tola somehow managed to find a way around the eons old law?* He shuddered to think of the consequences if true.

Reima closed up the café and went upstairs, waiting for Teegan to return. He took off his apron and changed into jeans and a T-shirt in preparation to go look for her. Teegan entered through the back door. She locked the door and stared through the small window.

"There you are." Reima sighed in relief. "I was worried. Where did you go?"

"Tola's not the only one with spies." Teegan turned with a frown.

Without another word or further explanation, Teegan went into her room and locked the door.

II

Aubree sat in the living room with Ariana and Elliot watching a movie. Aubree had still not arranged a time for them to meet Reima, and Ariana wondered if Aubree even mentioned it to him. She had not gone out with him since the previous week, though they often sent each other texts. Elliot grew impatient about meeting this boy, and even suggested that he and Ariana go down to the café while Aubree was in school.

"That wouldn't be fair," said Ariana at the time. "There's still plenty of time before her birthday. I trust Aubree. Be patient."

Aubree's phone rang just as the credits started rolling on their movie.

"It's Reima." She took her phone to her bedroom to answer it, but came out only a moment later. "His dog just had puppies. Can I go over and see them? Please?"

Ariana looked over at Elliot. He nodded.

"Sure. In fact, I think this may be the perfect opportunity for us to meet him." Ariana's raised eyebrows said it was not a request.

"Reima?" Aubree said into the phone. "They said I can come over, but they want to meet you. Is it okay if they come too? Great! I'll see you soon!" Aubree hung up her phone and ran back to her bedroom. "Hurry and get ready!" she called from her room.

"What's the rush?" asked Elliot. "It's not like the puppies are going anywhere."

"Just hurry!"

Ariana and Elliot smiled at each other and went to get dressed. A crash sounded from Aubree's room.

"I'm okay!" Aubree yelled down the hall. "My laundry basket just fell over!"

Ariana chuckled and shook her head. "She seems excited."

"Just a little bit," agreed Elliot.

Ariana put on a plain yellow blouse and black pants. She brushed her hair and teeth then followed Elliot out of the bedroom. Aubree waited by the front door, her hand on the doorknob. She opened the door at her sister and brother-in-law's approach and ushered them outside.

"Reima and Teegan live above the café." Aubree walked ahead of the other two.

"Who's Teegan?" asked Elliot.

"Reima's business partner," explained Aubree.

"Oh," said Ariana. "Is she the tall, dark-haired woman usually running the pastry counter?"

Aubree nodded. "She seems scary at first, but she's really cool."

"They live together?" asked Elliot, raising an eyebrow to Ariana.

They arrived at the café and walked around to the back of the building, to the stairs leading to the apartment. Aubree knocked on the door.

"It's open," answered Reima from inside.

Aubree opened the door; Ariana and Elliot followed her inside. Reima and Teegan sat cross-legged on the floor. A border collie laid on a pile of blankets in front of them, nursing a litter of puppies.

Reima stood and hugged Aubree.

"You must be Ariana and Elliot." He turned to them. "I've heard a lot about you. I'm Reima."

"Yes, we have heard a lot about you, too," said Elliot. Aubree blushed.

"This is my business partner and roommate, Teegan."

Teegan came over to shake their hands.

"Do I know you from somewhere?" Teegan asked Ariana. "You look kind of familiar."

"I've been in the café a few times," replied Ariana, "and I work at Cupid's Hands, the flower shop a few blocks down."

"It must be from the café." Teegan shook her head. "I've never been inside a flower shop."

"Let's go see the puppies." Aubree sat down on the floor in front of the dog. "How many are there?"

"Five." Reima sat beside her and pointed out the puppies as he spoke. "Three girls and two boys."

"Please, have a seat." Teegan gestured to the couch. "Make yourselves at home. Do you want anything to drink?"

"Just water please." Ariana sat down on the couch.

"Make it two." Elliot sat beside Ariana.

Teegan nodded and walked into the kitchen. "Aubree? You want anything?"

"Do you have any soda?" asked Aubree.

Teegan came back in and handed them their drinks.

"Have you named the puppies yet?" asked Aubree.

Reima shook his head. "Not yet. We were waiting for you."

While Aubree and Reima discussed names, Ariana's eye fell on a painting of a dragon, the only decoration in the apartment that Ariana could see. She stood and walked closer to examine it. The painting gave her a strange feeling, almost as if the painting were alive. Freedom and pride showed through the emerald eyes of the dragon, intense strength in the curve of its black wings. Ariana felt the power flowing through the dragon's silent roar, almost smelled the sulfur.

"I see you like my painting." Teegan walked up behind her.

Ariana turned. "I do. Where did you get it?"

"Oh, I've had that for years," Teegan touched the painting with reverence, as if she touched a memory.

Ariana stiffened. *It is a memory. Hers.* The dragon's eyes in the painting were the same as the eyes in the woman beside her. This was not a painting of a dragon from some artist's imagination, this was a portrait.

Ariana gasped and took a step back.

Teegan looked at her with confusion. "Is something wrong?"

Ariana composed herself. "No," she smiled. "I just lost my balance." She went back to the couch.

"Are you okay?" asked Elliot.

Ariana smiled and put a hand on his knee. "I'm fine."

I cannot tell him here. Not with Aubree in the room. If Teegan is fae, then Reima most likely is as well. Ariana felt Teegan's eyes on her, watching. Ariana hid her unease by leaning her head on Elliot's shoulder. *Does she suspect that Elior and I are not human? If she looks into my eyes, she'll know for sure.* Ariana glanced at Reima and Aubree, still focused on naming the puppies.

Reima nodded in approval to Aubree's final name suggestion, then stood. He walked over to the couch.

"Aubree said you wanted to talk to me?"

"Yes," said Elliot. "Is there somewhere we can talk privately?"

"Sure, we can talk in my room." Reima pointed down the hall.

"Great." Elliot stood and started to follow Reima. "Ariana?" he asked. She still sat on the couch. "Are you coming?"

"You go ahead." Ariana waved him on. "You know what we wanted to tell him. There's no need for both of us to be in there."

She smiled and hoped no one would press her further. She wanted to join them, to find out Reima's true heritage, but she did not want to leave Aubree alone with a dragon. *Especially since there is a good change Teegan is an exile.*

"Alright." Elliot followed Reima down the hall.

Teegan sat on the couch beside Ariana after they left the room.

"You don't have to be worried about me hurting Aubree." Teegan spoke in a quiet voice that Aubree could not overhear.

"I didn't say I was." Ariana avoided Teegan's eyes.

"You didn't have to," said Teegan. Ariana did not look up. "You know, hiding your eyes gives away just as much as letting someone see them."

Ariana looked up.

"Don't worry," said Teegan. "I won't say anything."

"Is Reima—" Ariana began.

Teegan nodded. "Not a dragon, though."

"What are you two whispering about?" asked Aubree.

"Nothing," smiled Ariana. "We were just getting to know each other." She wanted to know more about this dragon, but she could not say anything else with Aubree listening.

Aubree rolled her eyes, telling Ariana she did not buy the explanation. "I'm not a baby anymore, Ana. I can tell when you're hiding something, but I'll let it go, because I want you to come look at the puppies."

Ariana shook her head and knelt down beside her sister.

"Is this just a ploy to convince me to let you keep one?" she asked.

Aubree grinned. "Unashamedly. Just look at them. They're so cute and tiny."

"They are cute," admitted Ariana, "but they won't stay tiny. You know that, right? One day, each of these puppies will be as big as their mother."

Aubree nodded. "I know, but we have a big enough house. And we have a nice yard for him to run around in."

Ariana chuckled. "Him? This sounds like you've already picked one out."

Aubree grinned again and pointed to one of the puppies. A gray one with black and white speckles.

"Ariana?" Elliot asked from behind them. She turned. "I'm done talking to Reima, but he's still waiting in his room in case there's anything you wanted to add."

"There is, actually," Ariana nodded and stood.

Aubree looked up with a worried expression and Ariana kissed her on top of her head to help ease her concern.

"Aubree will probably try to convince you to let her have a puppy," Ariana added to Elliot. "Don't let her sweet-talk you into agreement until we can discuss it."

"Do you really think I'm that weak?" asked Elliot.

"I've known you for a long time, my love," answered Ariana, kissing his cheek.

She walked to the room Elliot indicated.

Reima sat on his bed, waiting. "Elliot told me the ground rules. They are fair rules. I would never do anything to her."

Ariana nodded. "I believe you. I do have one question, though." She sat on the bed and faced him.

"What is it?" asked Reima.

Ariana looked Reima in the eye, letting him see hers as she did so. Reima sat up straighter, backing away in surprise.

"You—You're a—" Reima stammered.

"Why were you banished?" asked Ariana, interrupting him.

"I'm a wolf," admitted Reima. "My father is the alpha of my former pack. He was punishing another member for some minor infraction, but he was getting out of hand with it. I stepped in to stop him before he killed the other one, and he banished me from the pack. He took me to King Nikolam, of Cinna, who exiled me to the Mortal Realm."

Ariana silently contemplated Reima's story. When animal fae came through the Veil, they came out on the other side in either human form, or their animal form, and while in general, the more dangerous ones came through as animals, this was not always the case. Reima, however, did not strike Ariana as dangerous. On the contrary, she knew wolves were only attracted to one person in their entire lives, and, thus, he would do anything to keep Aubree from harm.

"Aubree doesn't know," she said, at last. "Aubree *can't* know what we are, what she is. I can't tell you why, right now, but I am asking you to keep it secret for now."

"I promise not to say anything until you give me permission." Reima touched two fingers to the place where his left wolf ear would be, the canine sign that accompanied a vow. "I'm just relieved to find out that Aubree isn't mortal."

Ariana chuckled. "I'm sure you are."

Reima looked down, embarrassed.

"As long as you treat Aubree right, you have nothing to fear from either Elliot or me," promised Ariana. "I do have to ask, Teegan's not dangerous, is she?"

Reima firmly shook his head. "Only to her enemies. She's a good person. She's like the older sister I never had."

Ariana sighed in relief. "Thank you. That makes me feel much better. There was one more thing I wanted to discuss with you."

Reima chuckled. "You're wondering if Aubree can have one of the puppies?"

"How did you –"

"She's been telling me how badly she wants a dog, and she's had a plan, ever since I told her I had a pregnant dog in my apartment, to convince you to let her keep a puppy."

"Of course she did," chuckled Ariana. "She already has one picked out."

"I know," laughed Reima. "She named him Winston."

"Yes, that sounds like a name she would pick," laughed Ariana. "Anyway, I was thinking, her birthday is in two months, and the puppies should be old enough by then. Perhaps the puppy could be a birthday present."

"Sounds like a plan," agreed Reima.

"Of course, I will have to check with Elliot, but I have no doubt he'll agree," said Ariana. "I will let you know our final decision soon."

Aubree grew worried. Ariana and Reima had talked for a long time, far longer than he and Elliot had talked. Ariana and Reima finally came back into the living room. Ariana silently sat on the couch beside Elliot.

"Well?" Aubree looked from Ariana to Reima. "What did you talk about? You were in there for a while."

Ariana shook her head. "If we wanted you to hear it, we would have spoken in here. All you need to know is that Reima has agreed to the boundaries we set."

Aubree smiled, smug. "I told you he would."

"We never said we thought he wouldn't," said Elliot.

Ariana raised an eyebrow at him.

Elliot shrugged. "Well it's true. I never said it to *her*, and I never actually thought he wouldn't. I was just, preparing you for the possibility that he wouldn't."

"Whatever you say, Darling." Ariana kissed him on the cheek.

Reima knelt beside Aubree and she smiled.

"So? What do you think of my family?" asked Aubree.

"I like them," answered Reima, "and they seem to like me."

"How could they not?" answered Aubree. "You're amazing."

Reima smiled. "I wish everyone thought that way."

They stayed at Reima's for another hour, until Elliot announced that it was time to go.

"It's getting late," he said. "Aubree has school tomorrow, and the rest of us have work."

Ariana and Elliot said goodbye to Teegan and Reima then stepped outside to wait for Aubree. Teegan hugged Aubree and disappeared into her room, leaving Reima and Aubree alone.

"I'm really glad Ariana and Elliot approve of you," said Aubree. "Not that I was worried they wouldn't, it's just—I'm happy they do."

Reima chuckled. "Me too."

"So, um, are hugs allowed in the boundaries they set?" asked Aubree.

"As a matter of fact, they are."

Aubree went in for a hug and did not let go until Ariana knocked from outside to let her know they still waited.

"I guess I'll see you after school tomorrow." Aubree pulled away.

Reima nodded. "Definitely."

He seemed much more relaxed after talking with Elliot and Ariana. He opened the door and Aubree smiled at him as she followed her sister and brother-in-law down the stairs.

Two months is going to be a long time, she thought.

"Okay, what's the part you're not telling me?" asked Elliot once Ariana got into bed later that night.

"What do you mean?" she asked.

"At the apartment. You were acting strangely and I figured it was something you didn't want to mention in front of Aubree, but not something bad enough to cause you to change your mind about her spending time over there. Plus, you gave me your 'I'll tell you later' look."

"Oh, that." Ariana rolled and faced him. "It's not that I wasn't going to tell you, I just didn't want to say it there."

"I think that's what I just said."

"I don't think it's a big deal," began Ariana, "but Reima and Teegan are faeries."

Elliot thoughtfully nodded. "Mmm, yeah, I thought so. It struck me as kind of odd that they didn't have any family pictures or anything. That makes sense if they're faeries. Did you find out what kind?"

"Yes. Teegan is a dragon, and Reima is a wolf." Ariana prepared herself for Elliot's objections.

"I can see that."

"You're not upset?" asked Ariana. "I thought you might think they're too dangerous or something."

"Not if you don't," he said. "You're a pretty good judge of character. Besides, I actually feel safer with a dragon and a wolf on our side. In case—well, you know."

"Yes, I know." Ariana snuggled close to Elliot and he put his arms around her. "I feel the same way. I just hope it never comes to that."

Elliot kissed her on top of her head. "Me either."

12

School and homework kept Aubree busy in the weeks leading up to her sixteenth birthday. She spent much of her free time with Reima. Marcia often accompanied Aubree to the café after school to do their homework, and to keep Aubree from flirting too much. Reima, and even Teegan, stopped by their table during free moments to help them if they needed it.

Ariana invited Reima and Teegan over for dinner at least once a week. Ariana and Teegan grew into close friends. She was at their house as often as Reima, if not more so. Aubree eagerly awaited the arrival of her birthday and the ability to spend time alone with Reima.

Teegan offered the café to host Aubree's party. Aubree and Marcia walked straight there after school. Marcia lingered outside her locker and made Aubree take the long way to the café to give Aubree's school friends time to get there first. They found everyone waiting.

Reima greeted Aubree with a hug as soon as she and Marcia walked through the glass doors. They decorated the café with purple and blue balloons; table cloths of the same colors covered the tables. A "Happy Birthday!" banner hung across the back wall and a small pile of gifts sat on the pastry counter.

"Happy birthday," said Reima.

Aubree smiled. "Thank you."

"You know? I almost didn't believe you when you first told me about Reima," said Lisa, one of Aubree's school friends, "but you were right. He's gorgeous."

Aubree blushed and Reima looked down, his hair hiding his embarrassed smile. Aubree kept hold of Reima's hand as she walked through the café to where Ariana and Elliot spoke with her aunts. She greeted her friends as made her way through the crowd.

"Happy birthday, Aubree." Ariana hugged her sister.

Aubree smiled. "This place looks great."

"That is thanks to me." Teegan walked up behind Aubree. She draped one arm across Aubree's shoulder and the other across Reima's shoulder. Aubree did not try to shrug her off this time, she had grown accustomed to it. "Ariana was kind of freaking out about having people in your house."

"Yeah, she does that every year," laughed Aubree. "She's kind of a neat-freak."

"Which is why I cannot, for the life of me, figure out where your sloppiness comes from." Ariana playfully sighed and shook her head.

"I'm not sloppy in everything," protested Aubree. "I just don't understand why my room has to stay clean all the time if I'm the only one spending any time in there."

"But you're not the only one who spends time there." Marcia playfully nudged Aubree. "What about when I come over?"

"Like your room is any better?" interjected Aunt Claudette.

"Well, I think this is enough talk." Teegan walked toward the back room. "I'm ready to party."

Rock music blasted from the speakers.

Ariana rolled her eyes. "Teegan! We discussed this!" she yelled. The music lowered in volume.

"Spoilsport," muttered Teegan, re-entering the dining area.

Ariana smiled and shook her head.

"Go on, have fun," Elliot told Aubree. "Go introduce Reima to your friends."

Aubree smiled and dragged Reima around the room, bragging on him more than really introducing him.

She looked up when she heard the door. A tall, thin man entered. He wore brown dreadlocks that hung down to his chest. He nervously looked around the room until he saw Aubree and Reima and walked over to them. Aubree recognized him as the man Reima had asked to watch his stuff at that first picnic.

Reima smiled at his friend's approach. "Marvin! I'm glad you could come. This is Aubree."

Marvin smiled and nodded his head in greeting.

"I hope you don't mind that I invited him," said Reima. "I just wanted you to meet him, and to introduce him to Marcia."

"Oh!" Aubree forgot about telling Reima that Marcia asked if he had any friends. "No, that's fine. It's nice to meet you, Marvin."

Marvin handed Aubree a package wrapped in light-blue, balloon covered paper. "I didn't really know what to get you, but I didn't want to show up empty handed." He had a soft, melancholy voice, like wind blowing through the trees.

"Thank you." Aubree put the gift with the rest and then the three of them walked over to where Marcia stood by the snacks.

"Marcia," Aubree tapped her on the shoulder.

Marcia turned around. "Yeah?" she asked around a mouthful of potato chips, swallowing quickly when she saw Marvin.

"Aubree mentioned that you wanted me to introduce you to one of my friends." Reima gestured to the other man. "This is Marvin. He doesn't say much, but he likes to listen. I figured you would make a good match, since you like to talk. Marvin, this is Aubree's cousin, Marcia."

Marcia nervously chuckled while Marvin shyly hung his head.

"It's nice to meet you." Marvin glanced up at Marcia and she smiled.

"Ditto." Marcia gestured to an empty table. "Do you want to sit down?"

Marvin nodded, but walked around and pulled out the chair closest to Marcia first. Marcia glanced at Aubree and Reima with raised eyebrows. She smiled and sat down.

"We'll just leave you two to get to know each other," chuckled Aubree.

"Who wants cake?" Ariana called.

The whole party gathered around as Teegan came out of the kitchen, carrying a giant, chocolate chip cupcake with sixteen candles on top.

"Make a wish." Elliot lit the candles.

Aubree thought for a minute. "I don't have to. I already have everything I could wish for." She smiled up at Reima.

Ariana laid a hand on Aubree's shoulder. "Then just make a small wish. Those are more likely to come true, anyway."

"Just make sure it's a good one," added Teegan. "Birthday wishes are powerful. You really don't want to waste them."

Aubree smiled and closed her eyes. She thought about wishing for a puppy; she heard them playing upstairs. She paused; a strange thought entered her head. *I wish I knew more about my parents.* She blew out the candles, all sixteen in one breath.

A strange chill ran down her spine and the smoke from the candles seemed to shimmer. The cheering of her friends brought her back to the present. Elliot cut the cake while Teegan served ice cream.

Ariana ensured everyone had a plate and told Aubree to open gifts. Aubree sat in a chair in front of the counter and opened what Ariana handed her. The first thing she opened was a make-up palette from Marcia.

"Don't worry, I got Ariana's permission first," she said.

Aubree smiled and thanked both Marcia and Ariana. Aubree got mostly clothes from her school friends, a new pair of boots and a set of headbands from Aunt Claudette, and a porcelain ballerina doll from Aunt Charity.

The next gift Ariana handed her was the package from Marvin. Aubree tore through the paper and found an old book bound in a strange black leather. Gold edged the pages. The book was incredibly old and in remarkably good shape. Aubree felt that she could handle it without worrying about tearing the pages.

Aubree flipped through it and saw intricately drawn pictures and carefully handwritten words. The book was written in a strange language, but the pictures told the stories.

"Why would you give this to me?" asked Aubree. "Not that I don't appreciate it, but it just feels, I don't know, special."

Marvin shrugged. "I've had that book a long time. It's just been sitting at my house, gathering dust. It needs a new home."

"Well, thank you." Aubree smiled and handed the book to Ariana to put with the rest. The pile of unopened gifts disappeared and Aubree had not received anything from Ariana and Elliot, or from Reima.

Reima cleared his throat. "I guess it's my turn now." He got out of his chair and walked over to stand beside Aubree, turned where he could face her and the rest of the guests at the same time. He took her hand. "Aubree, my gift to you is more of a question." Aubree blushed, already knowing what he was going to ask. "You're sixteen now, and I have Ariana and Elliot's permission to ask this. Will you be my girlfriend?"

Aubree grinned and nodded. A chorus of "Awwwwww!" echoed from the crowd. Aubree stuck her tongue out.

"Kiss him!" Marcia called out.

Aunt Claudette shushed her.

"I think they should save the kissing for later." Elliot shot Aubree and Reima a warning look. "Much later. She's not done with her presents."

"Sharing a first kiss would be a great gift, I think." Teegan teased with a wink.

"Teegan," growled Reima, without looking at her. The word more of a warning than anything else. "I actually do have something else," he said to Aubree.

Reima reached into the pocket of his jacket and pulled out a small silver box, tied with a black string. Aubree untied the string and opened the box. Inside was a gold necklace in the shape of a wolf, howling at an abalone-shell moon.

"It's beautiful." Aubree gently touched the necklace. "Will you help me put it on?"

"Does this mean you're saying yes to being my girlfriend?" he asked, fastening the necklace behind her.

"What do you think?" she asked, hugging him.

"Okay, you have one more gift," said Ariana. "Close your eyes while I go get it."

Aubree squeezed her eyes shut. The muffled squeals of her friends, and the unmistakable sound of panting, told Aubree what it was even before she opened her eyes.

"Okay, you can open your eyes now." Ariana placed a fat, cuddly puppy in Aubree's lap.

"Winston!" Aubree squealed in delight as the puppy licked her face. She looked up at Ariana and Elliot. "Thank you!"

Ariana smiled. "You're welcome."

"Now, don't forget, Winston is your responsibility," said Elliot. "Walking him, feeding him, house training him, all of that is on you."

"We already have all the supplies at the house," added Ariana.

Aubree nuzzled her face into Winston's furry tummy.

"You guys want to see him?" asked Aubree.

The words barely left her lips and the crowd surged, surrounding her and the puppy. They petted Winston and asked to hold him. Winston wagged his tail and kissed anyone who came near.

The party wound down and the guests left, one by one.

"Happy birthday, Aubree," said Marvin. "Thank you for letting me stay. Enjoy the book."

Aubree nodded. "Thank you for coming. It was nice to meet you."

Marvin smiled and nodded. He turned and went to exchange phone numbers with Marcia. Aubree looked for Ariana to see if they would have to leave, too, and saw her in deep conversation with Elliot, Aunt Claudette, and Aunt Charity. Aunt Claudette nodded at something Ariana said and Elliot broke away from the group. He walked over to Aubree and Reima.

"Is it time to go?" asked Aubree.

Elliot shook his head. "Not quite yet. We need to talk."

"About what?" Aubree immediately felt nervous.

"Not here," said Elliot. "Upstairs. Both of you."

"Am I in trouble?" asked Reima. "I followed all your rules."

"You're not in trouble," Elliot smiled and squeezed Reima's shoulder reassuringly. "This has nothing to do with your relationship."

Aubree let out a breath she did not know she held, but the nervous feeling in her stomach still did not go away. The feeling intensified when Aunt Claudette, Aunt Charity, and Marcia followed Ariana and Teegan upstairs. Aubree heard Marcia ask Aunt Claudette what was going on, but she did not hear a response. Aubree wanted to take Reima's hand for comfort, but she needed both arms to carry Winston. Reima seemed to sense what she wanted because he put a hand on her shoulder as they walked up the stairs.

Winston wiggled when he saw his mother and siblings. Aubree put him down and he ran over and jumped on one of his sisters that Aubree named Sunny. Aubree wanted to stand there and watch the puppies playing instead of hearing what Elliot had to say, but she felt Reima gently guide her to the sofa. Her stomach somersaulted. Aubree chewed on the inside of her bottom lip and sat down. She clasped her hands to keep from fidgeting.

Why do I get the feeling my entire life is about to be turned upside down?

"Do you know what's going on?" whispered Marcia, sitting down beside Aubree.

"No idea," Aubree whispered back.

Ariana sat down in one of the chairs, Elliot stood beside her. Teegan locked both doors, at Ariana's request, then dragged more chairs in from the dining room for Aunt Charity and Aunt Claudette. Ariana opened her mouth and then closed it. Elliot put his hand on her shoulder.

"I don't really know where to begin." Ariana's eyes filled with tears. "How do you say something that could potentially ruin someone's life?"

"Ruin whose life?" asked Marcia. "Mama, what's going on?"

Aunt Claudette glanced over at Ariana, and took over speaking. She looked straight at Marcia and Aubree.

"First off, I want you both to listen carefully to what we are going to tell you," said Aunt Claudette. "The things you're about to hear may sound unbelievable at first, but they're true. Every word." She took a deep breath. "Marcia, Aubree, we have been keeping something from you. Something rather large and important, but we only kept this from you to protect you."

"Kept what from us?" asked Aubree.

"There is no easy way to say this, so I'll just say it. We are not human," said Aunt Claudette.

"What? What do you mean we're not human?" asked Marcia. "What are we then?"

"Faeries," said Aunt Charity.

The room fell silent.

Faeries? An image of tiny, winged women flashed through Aubree's mind. She shook it away. *Clearly, that's not what Aunt Charity means.* Aubree looked from Reima to Teegan. *They don't look fazed at all. Do they already know? Are they faeries, too?* Aubree put a hand to her forehead, suddenly lightheaded. *It's true, though. I don't know how, but I know it's true. I can feel it.*

Marcia vigorously shook her head, hitting Aubree in the face with her hair. Aubree blinked back to reality and stared at her cousin.

"What!" Marcia derisively laughed "Faeries? You have *got* to be kidding me!"

"Please, keep your voice down, dear," said Aunt Claudette.

"But we *can't* be faeries." Marcia leaned forward. "There's no such things! Besides, if we were faeries, then how come we don't all have wings and wands and leave glitter trails wherever we go?"

"We're not pixies," Teegan snapped in annoyance.

Aubree stared at the woman. *At least she is one.* She glanced at Reima. *What about him?*

"Oh! You're one too?" Marcia crossed her arms and glared at Teegan. "What about Reima? Is he a faerie too? Are everyone we know faeries?"

"What kind of faeries are we?" asked Aubree, cutting off Marcia. She looked at Aubree in shock

Ariana spoke. "You, Marcia, Charity, Claudette, Elliot, and I are elves."

Marcia scoffed.

"Be quiet," Aunt Claudette scolded her.

"Elves are like two inches tall and sew shoes!" scoffed Marcia.

"Some," agreed Aunt Charity, "but not our kind."

"Our kind do not look much different from the way we look now," said Aunt Claudette.

"What about Reima and Teegan?" asked Aubree. "What kind of faeries are they?"

"Take a guess." Teegan walked over to stand beside the painting on the wall and cocked her head to one side, making the tattoo on her neck stand out.

Aubree looked from the tattoo to the painting and back to Teegan. Her eyes widened in realization.

"Yep," smirked Teegan, "I'm a dragon."

"Oh, please!" Marcia rolled her eyes.

"And you're a wolf, aren't you?" Aubree asked Reima.

"How did you know?" asked Reima.

Aubree smiled and brushed the hair off of his face. "Your eyes."

"You're not seriously buying this, are you?" asked Marcia.

Aubree turned to her. "It's true, Marcia. Can't you feel it?"

Marcia curtly shook her head. "I don't feel anything. Prove it."

Aunt Claudette sighed. "We can't prove it. Here in the Mortal Realm, our faerie abilities are suppressed."

"How convenient."

"That is *enough!*" shouted Aunt Claudette. "We are here to discuss something important and potentially life-threatening. If you are going to continue to challenge what is being said, then you are forbidden to speak at all. You will sit there, with your mouth closed, while Ariana is speaking. If I hear one more word from you then you will be grounded from now until the day you move out. Is that clear?"

Aubree leaned back against Reima. She had never seen her aunt this angry before. Marcia folded her arms across her chest and slumped back against the sofa. Aunt Claudette cleared her throat and looked at Ariana, encouraging her to continue.

"Thank you, Claudette," said Ariana. "Well, I guess the next thing you should know is that Claudette and Charity aren't really our aunts. Aubree, you were only a baby when we came through the Veil, and Claudette came with us as a wet-nurse. Charity was already here and we stayed with her. Claudette's husband—your father, Marcia—had to stay behind."

Marcia glanced up at Ariana, and then at her mother, but stayed silent.

"Why did we leave?" asked Aubree.

Ariana sighed. "That is the hard part. Before I go on, I need everyone to swear not to say anything to anyone about this. If any of what I am about to say gets out, then all of our lives would be in danger."

Everyone agreed. Ariana continued.

"First of all, my name is not Ariana," said Ariana. "That is the name I chose for myself when we arrived here in order to hide my true identity. My true name is Eirian, Princess of the Kingdom of Varia."

Teegan straightened and stepped away from the wall.

"Come again?" she asked in surprise. "No wonder I thought you looked familiar."

Reima's eyes widened in surprise, and he tensed, but did not say anything.

"You're a princess?" asked Aubree.

Ariana nodded. "So are you. Our parents are King Alberic and Queen Livia of Varia."

Ariana paused to give Aubree time to process the news. Marcia looked dying to say something, but held her tongue.

"Is Aubree my real name?" asked Aubree.

"Yes. You were allowed to keep your real name, since your birth was never announced. Your name would not give us away," said Ariana. "However, Elliot's true name is Elior."

Aubree nodded. "Go on. What happened?"

"Several months before you were born, before our parents even knew that Mama was pregnant, a fae woman, named Tola, came to me," continued Ariana. "She is extremely dangerous, and very powerful. Her power is great enough, that many people are willing to ignore the danger she poses for the chance she might help them with problems they cannot solve on their own.

"Our father was one of those people. When I was born, I was very sick. Daddy was afraid I would die, and nothing else worked. He went to Tola for help. She agreed to heal me, but Daddy did not realize that what Tola wanted in return was you, Aubree. That is what Tola came to me about before you were born."

Aubree's blood ran cold and she moved closer to Reima. He protectively wrapped an arm around her.

"That's why we had to leave, to protect me?" asked Aubree.

Ariana nodded. "We had to keep it a secret. The fewer people who knew, the better. That's why we never mentioned it to you or to Marcia."

"So, why tell us now?" asked Aubree.

"You're sixteen now," said Ariana. "I never planned on keeping this a secret forever. Honestly, I didn't think we would be here this long."

Aubree thoughtfully nodded. "I know I should be surprised, but it all makes sense. It answers questions I've been too afraid to ask."

Ariana smiled in relief.

"I have something to add to that." Teegan's voice sounded odd, tight, almost as though her throat was closing in. "A couple months ago, one of Tola's spies came into the café. I tracked him down and tried to find out what he was looking for. All I found out was that Tola was looking for someone. Someone who ran away instead of paying Tola what she was due."

Ariana gasped and muttered something in a strange language. Aubree sometimes heard her and Elliot use it when they thought she was not listening. Ariana leaned closer to Elliot, taking his hand.

"She's here?" asked Ariana.

"I don't think she's on this side of the Veil yet," said Teegan. "She's just sent out spies. If she knew you were here, she would have done something already."

"What are we going to do?" asked Aubree.

"I don't think we should do anything," said Marcia. Claudette started to scold her. "No, hear me out," she said before her mother could say anything. "If she doesn't know where we are yet, then we don't have anything to worry about. It means that the plan you guys made years ago is still working. The surest way to make her find us is to change our plans. If we try to run or hide, then she'll know who we are and come after us."

"We just act like nothing's changed?" asked Ariana.

"It's actually quite a sound plan." Claudette proudly smiled at her daughter.

Aubree turned to Marcia. "I thought you didn't believe in any of this."

Marcia shrugged. "I don't, but you all seem pretty convinced about it. I figure I'll just go along with it, for now."

Aubree smiled and hugged her former cousin.

Ariana nodded. "Then it's settled. We don't change anything. We keep going on like we have for the past sixteen years."

"I still think we need some kind of plan in case she finds us," said Elliot.

"If she finds you, then come to the café," suggested Reima. "We'll hide you up here."

"Won't that be kind of obvious, though?" Marcia raised an eyebrow. "I mean, we're here all the time already."

"I'll keep an eye on the spies," offered Teegan. "See how close they are to finding you, and warn you ahead of time if anything changes."

"If that happens, then I'll contact Daddy and get him to send guards over," said Ariana. "She'll be easier to fight here where she can't use her powers."

Teegan spoke up again. "Actually, she's found a way to keep many of her powers."

Eyes filled with surprise and fear, turned to Teegan.

"What? How did she do that?" asked Claudette.

"I don't know, but I will try to find out," promised Teegan. "Don't worry, Reima and I will keep your secret. We'll keep you safe."

"What does she want with Aubree, anyway?" asked Reima.

Ariana shook her head. "I've been asking myself the same question for sixteen years. I still don't have an answer."

Ariana could not sleep that night. Fear of waking in the Razor Wood kept her eyes open. She tried not to wake Elliot by tossing and turning. She finally got out of bed and went into the kitchen to make herself a cup of tea. She sat at the table, sipping her tea, and stared at her reflection in the back-door window. The face she saw, the one she came to know, differed greatly from the young Elf princess that stared back at her in another lifetime. Eirian was happy and carefree. She had all of eternity to figure out her life. The expression on Ariana's face showed someone who had to grow up much sooner than planned. Though her faerie blood prevented any signs of aging from appearing on her face, one only needed to look into her eyes to see the truth.

"I want to go home," she whispered to the glass. "I want things to go back to the way they were." Tears sprang to her eyes and slid down her cheeks.

"I know you do," whispered Elliot from behind her. "I do too."

Ariana jumped at the sudden voice. "I thought you were asleep." She sniffed and wiped at her eyes.

Elliot hugged her from behind. "I felt you get up. I was worried."

Ariana stood, turned, and buried her face in Elliot's chest. Tears freely flowed down her face. "I don't like this. I don't like doing nothing. I don't like hiding, and I don't like running. I don't know what to do, but I don't want to keep doing what we have been doing. I just want it to be over," she started sobbing. "I want to take Aubree and go home and pretend like none of this ever happened. I want to crawl into bed and never get out. I want to punch Tola in her smug face. I don't want to be afraid to sleep. I want to be happy again. I thought I was okay, but telling Aubree, and finding out that Tola has sent out spies, just made it all real again."

Elliot stroked her hair and let her rant. "If you come up with a solid plan, I will support you one hundred percent. In the meantime, I think you're right. We can't just sit here and do nothing. We need to let your parents know what has happened."

"But they told us not to contact them."

"I know they did, but that was before Tola started looking for us here."

"I'll tell Claudette and Charity tomorrow," said Ariana.

13

"I'll get it!" Aubree called from the living room. She ran to the front door and pulled it open.

"Are you ready for an epic sleep over?" asked Marcia.

Aubree laughed and helped Marcia carry her stuff inside. "You say that every time you come over. Most of the time we just end up watching movies in the living room."

"Hey, that can be epic," pouted Marcia.

Ariana suggested to Charity and Claudette that someone needed to go back to the Faerie Realm and update their parents on recent events. Claudette volunteered with a cover story she would be at an out-of-state conference and gone most of the week. Marcia would stay at Aubree's for school.

The girls carried Marcia's stuff to Aubree's room. Aubree opened her bedroom door and Winston barked and ran up to them.

"There's the puppy," cooed Marcia. "Who's a good boy? Who's a cute little puppy?"

Winston rolled over and whimpered at Marcia to rub his tummy.

Ariana announced her presence by knocking on the open door. "I'm assuming you girls are going to spend the night in the living room again. I thought about ordering pizza tonight, instead of cooking."

"Yes, please!" answered both girls simultaneously.

"What toppings?" asked Ariana.

"That depends." Aubree turned to Ariana. "How many pizzas are you getting?"

"Two, one for you two and one for Elliot and me."

"I want bacon and extra cheese," said Aubree.

"And I want mushrooms, extra cheese, and black olives," added Marcia.

"Oh! I want olives, too!"

"Extra cheese and olives on the whole thing, mushrooms on one half, and bacon on the other," clarified Ariana. "Got it." She left the room to go order.

"Alright! Down to business. The plan for tonight is for me to teach you how to wear make-up. We want you to be irresistible to Reima on our double-date tomorrow night." Marcia picked up her bright pink make-up box and sat with it on the bed. "Where's that make-up palette I got you for your birthday?"

Aubree blushed as she got the palette from off her dresser and handed to Marcia.

"You haven't opened it yet?" asked Marcia in surprise.

Aubree shrugged. "My birthday was only a few days ago. Plus, you said you'd show me how to put it on. I was waiting for you."

"Oh, well I guess that's okay then."

Aubree spent the next thirty minutes sitting on her bed while Marcia tried out combinations of eyeshadow, lipstick, and blush to see which ones would look best.

"Lucky for you, we have just about the same complexion. This shouldn't be too hard." Marcia added the finishing touches on her current look. "There. What do you think?"

She held out a hand mirror to Aubree. Aubree looked at the mirror and then up at Marcia in surprise.

"What is this?" she exclaimed. "I look like a clown!"

"It doesn't look that bad," said Marcia. "But if you really don't like it, then go clean it off, and I'll try something else." She handed Aubree a bottle of make-up remover and a bag of cotton pads.

Aubree washed her face and returned to her room. Marcia tried again.

Aubree looked in the mirror again. "Now, it doesn't look like I'm wearing anything."

"Yeah, I went for a more natural look this time."

"Then what's the point of wearing make-up at all?"

"My thoughts exactly." Ariana poked her head into the room. "That's why I don't wear any and why I never bought you any. We don't need it."

Marcia tapped her chin. "Hmm, let me try something different, then."

"Later," said Ariana. "Pizza's here."

Aubree went to the bathroom, washed her face, and joined Marcia in the living room where Ariana had set out their pizza.

"Where exactly are you girls going on this double date tomorrow night?" asked Ariana.

"Some big fancy Italian restaurant that Marvin used to work at." Marcia shrugged her shoulders. "I can't remember the name of it."

"Okay, I'll ask Reima or Marvin when they come to pick you up tomorrow. You girls have fun tonight. Elliot and I will be in our room watching television. If you need anything, just shout."

Ariana hugged the girls and then walked to her room with the second pizza box.

Marcia took a slice of pizza from her half and took a bite. "Mmm! I love pizza." A string of melted cheese dangled from the corner of her mouth.

"Marcia, you kind of have..." Aubree laughed and gestured to Marcia's mouth.

Marcia giggled and wiped off the cheese. She picked up a stray mushroom that had fallen into the box and popped it into her mouth.

Aubree made a face. "I don't see how you can eat those."

"Like this." Marcia pulled another mushroom off her pizza and deliberately bit into it. "Mmmmmm! Delicious."

"You're crazy," laughed Aubree.

"And you're not?" laughed Marcia. "You still believe we're all faeries."

Aubree stopped laughing.

"I'm sorry," said Marcia. "I didn't mean to upset you, but, faeries? Seriously?"

"Haven't you ever noticed that there's something strange about us?" asked Aubree. "I mean, look around. There are pictures of us all over the room." Aubree pointed to the mantle. "See? There's Ariana and Elliot and me when I was ten. There's one with all of us when I was still a baby. Here's Ariana and Elliot on their wedding day. Don't you notice anything strange?"

Marcia shook her head. "Not really."

"Look harder." Aubree picked up the picture from when she was a baby and the one where she was ten. She handed them to Marcia. "Look."

Marcia sighed and looked at the pictures.

"What am I looking at?" she asked. "There's nothing strange about them, they look exactly the same!"

"That's my point," said Aubree. "They don't age."

"What are you talking about?"

"They don't age." Aubree pointed from the picture from when she was ten to the other one. "This one is ten whole years after this one, but Ariana and Elliot don't change at all. They look exactly the same in both of these pictures, and they still look the same today. The same goes for Aunt Charity and your mom, I mean, you and Aunt Claudette could be sisters."

Marcia stared at the pictures again. Her eyes widened. "Oh my gosh! You're right!" she exclaimed. "How have I not noticed this before?"

"Ana said that the Veil makes it so people don't notice." Aubree returned the pictures to the mantle. "Normal human beings will never notice unless the faerie points it out."

"But if we're not human, if we're—faeries, then how come we didn't notice?"

"Because we *thought* we were human," replied Aubree. "We would have noticed eventually, like when we stopped aging, but none of our friends would notice."

"When do we stop aging?" asked Marcia.

Aubree shook her head. "I'm not sure. I think it's somewhere in our mid-twenties, based off how old everyone else looks."

Marcia started laughing again; a different laugh from earlier. She emitted a high-pitched, almost panicky squeal that quickly turned into sobs.

Ariana and Elliot ran into the room.

"What happened?" asked Ariana.

Aubree held her arms around her friend. She looked up. "She realized that you were telling the truth."

Ariana sat down on the sofa and put a hand on Marcia's back.

"What made her believe?" asked Elliot.

"I showed her the pictures," said Aubree.

Marcia sniffled and looked up. "I'm sorry. This is all just so unreal. I mean, Aubree and Ariana are princesses and we're hiding from an evil witch? This is the kind of stuff that happens in fairy tales."

"Those stories had to come from somewhere," Ariana gently replied.

Marcia wiped her eyes. "I think I'm okay now. You know what? I think I actually remember the palace. I just thought I was imagining it. I mean, I was like, two when we left."

Aubree smiled. "I hope I get to see it soon. I bet it's beautiful."

"It is," agreed Ariana. "White trees with golden leaves surround the castle. The stones that make up the walls are flecked with silver. There's a fountain in the courtyard that I used to play in when I was little, and the play house Daddy had built for me." Tears filled Ariana's eyes. "That's where I first told Elliot I loved him and where we had our first kiss. There are so many things I wanted to show you."

"You'll be able to," said Aubree, "eventually."

Ariana smiled. "I know. I just wish you could have grown up there, with Mama and Daddy."

"Me, too," said Aubree. "Hey, at least I know that they're alive and I'm not an orphan like I previously thought."

That got a chuckle out of Ariana.

"Yes, that's true," she agreed. "That is very true."

"And I have a dad." Marcia closed her eyes. "Was—is he a guard or something?"

Ariana nodded. "He's the Captain of the Guard. His name is Devin. I'm sure your mom is telling him all about you right now."

"It's still strange to think about," said Marcia.

"It'll get easier with time," promised Ariana.

Hidden Identity

14

Reima knelt in front of his bed and peered into the darkness underneath, looking for his shoes. He sat back up. A low, frustrated growl rumbled in his throat. He stood and walked to the open closet, kicking aside a pile of dirty clothes.

Teegan knocked on his door. "Marvin's here."

"Thanks," said Reima. "Tell him I'll be out soon."

He spotted his shoes in the corner of the room, hiding under his work apron. He quickly put them on and went into the living room to meet Marvin. Since Reima did not have a car, they were going to take Marvin's car to pick up the girls for their double date.

"I'm ready," he said.

"About time." Teegan grabbed her bag and walked to the door.

"Where are you going?" asked Reima. "You can't crash our date."

Teegan stopped and put a hand on Reima's shoulder. "As much fun as that would be, that is not my plan. Tonight, anyway. Elliot has to help the church set up for some event there tomorrow morning and he'll be gone most of the night. With the girls going out with you two, that means Ariana has the house to herself and she invited me over for a night of cheesy chick-flicks and raw cookie dough."

Reima locked the door, and the three of them walked to Marvin's car.

"You hate chick-flicks," said Reima.

"I do," agreed Teegan. "I think they're stupid, but Ariana loves them, and she's my friend. Besides, she rejected all my ideas."

Reima laughed. "Well, I hope you enjoy yourself."

The drive to Aubree's house passed quickly, she only lived a few blocks from the café. Reima knocked on the door.

Ariana answered and invited them inside. "The girls are still getting ready." She stepped into the hallway that lead to the bedrooms. "Aubree, Marcia, your dates are here!"

One of the girls squeaked. Winston barked in reply.

"We're almost ready," Aubree called back. "Be quiet, Winston."

"Give us three minutes," added Marcia.

Ariana gestured to the living room. "Just make yourselves comfortable." She snapped her fingers and turned to Marvin. "Oh! What is the name of the restaurant you guys are going to? Marcia couldn't remember."

"Traverso's," responded Marvin. "It's my family's restaurant. My brother owns it now."

"Marcia couldn't remember your last name," Reima asked Marvin.

"I never told her my last name," shrugged Marvin.

Ariana turned to Teegan. "I was thinking about our plans tonight, and I think I came up with a compromise."

"I'm listening."

Ariana switched on the television and pointed with the remote to the description of a movie on the screen. "I found that today. It's got action and explosions, which you enjoy, and a compelling story line with a romantic aspect, which I'll enjoy. At least, that's what Elliot said."

"That sounds better than some sappy tear-jerker." Teegan flopped onto the couch, found the bowl of popcorn strategically placed on the coffee table, and popped a fistful into her mouth.

Marvin tapped Reima's arm and he looked up. The girls stood in the doorway. Marcia grinned and twirled, showing off a black, off-the-shoulder dress with a matching silk wrap. Aubree, in a teal knee-length dress with a scalloped bottom, nervously rubbed one bare arm. The top layer of her hair was pulled back and braided at the back, while the rest of her hair fell loose around her shoulders. She wore the necklace that Reima gave her around her neck.

"Wow," said Reima, his voice just above a whisper. "You look great."

Aubree smiled and tucked her hair behind one ear. "Thank you. You do, too."

Marvin smiled at Marcia. "I like your dress."

"Thanks, Marvin." Marcia threaded her arm through his.

Ariana held up her phone. "Elliot made me promise to get some pictures."

"Ana," Aubree groaned. "Come on, it's not like this is prom or anything."

"No, but it is your first official date." Ariana ushered everyone to the living room. "Come on, stand over there. You too, Marvin, Marcia."

The couples allowed Ariana to position them however she liked.

"I won't take many," Ariana promised. She snapped a handful of pictures and then allowed them to go.

"I locked Winston in my room so that he wouldn't jump on everyone," said Aubree as they walked out the door. "Can you let him back out, please?"

Ariana nodded. "Sure thing. You go and have fun. Oh, and Aubree, be careful. Don't do anything to draw attention to yourself."

"Don't worry, Ariana. Marvin and I will take care of them," promised Reima.

Aubree hugged Ariana goodbye and walked out to the car with Reima. Marvin and Marcia waited, already inside. Reima held the door open for Aubree and then got in on the other side.

Marcia took up the conversation baton and chattered away the whole time. Marvin would not have been able to get a word in if he wanted. From the look on his face and the way he glanced at Marcia as he drove, he seemed content to just listen. Reima looked over at Aubree. She rubbed her necklace between her fingers and listened to Marcia tell everyone about the dream she had the night before.

"What?" asked Aubree when she noticed Reima staring at her.

"Nothing." He shook his head. "You just look very beautiful."

Aubree self-consciously touched her hair. "It was mostly Marcia. She did my hair, lent me the dress, did my make-up, and painted my nails. If it weren't for her, I wouldn't look nearly this nice."

"That's not true." Reima took Aubree's hand. "You always look beautiful."

Aubree smiled. "Thank you."

The car stopped. Reima got out and walked around to open the door for Aubree. She smiled and took his outstretched hand. She clung to his arm as they walked across the parking lot.

"Ah, Marvin, it's good to see you again," said the hostess. "This must be your date. She's lovely."

Marvin introduced the group. "Marcia, this is Candice. Candice, this is Marcia, and this is my friend Reima and his girlfriend Aubree."

"Nice to meet you all. Your table is right over here. Tony saved you the best one." Candice led them to a relatively private table in a corner of the dining room.

Reima immediately felt self-conscious as he looked at the other diners in the room. He had never been in a place this fancy. The closest he ever came was the speakeasy Teegan ran when he first met her.

He pulled out Aubree's chair for her, noticing the crisp white tablecloth. In front of each chair sat an empty wine glass, three separate forks, and cloth napkins folded into odd shapes on top of the menus.

"I'll let Tony know you're here," said Candice and walked away.

"Who's Tony?" Marcia asked.

"The owner," answered Marvin.

"What exactly did you do when you worked here?" asked Aubree.

She did not seem at all fazed by the setup of the restaurant – bright, crystal chandeliers, expensive-looking marble statuettes decorating white glazed walls, and patrons dressed in fancy clothing.

Of course not. It's in her blood, thought Reima. *She is a princess, even if she did not know it until recently. I wonder how that will affect our relationship in the future. Ariana and Elliot did give me permission to be with her. It'll work out. I hope.*

"I was a waiter," said Marvin.

Marcia chuckled. "You must have been a really good waiter to get the attention of the owner."

"Tony's also my brother," Marvin stated matter-of-factly.

Marica turned to Marvin, mouth open in surprise. "Your brother owns this restaurant and you didn't tell me?"

Tony walked up to the table. "There's my little brother."

Tony had a loud, booming voice and thick black hair. He was short and stocky compared to Marvin, and when Marvin stood up to hug his brother, it seemed as if Tony could snap him in half.

"Hello, Tony," Marvin rubbed at his arms.

"And who is this lovely young lady?" asked Tony, taking Marcia's hand. "This can't be the girl you told me about. She's much too pretty to go with someone like you." Tony kissed the back of Marcia's hand.

"This is Marcia" Marvin awkwardly sat back down.

"Well, if you ever get bored with my little brother, you give me a call, eh?" Tony laughed and winked at Marcia.

Marvin closed his eyes and took a deep breath. Marcia sat, speechless for once.

"And who else do we have here?" asked Tony, oblivious to Marvin's discomfort.

"This is my friend Reima and his girlfriend, Aubree," said Marvin.

"Reima? That's kind of an odd name." Tony tilted his head in thought. "Where's it from?"

"My parents?" answered Reima.

"No, I meant, what nationality? Where is your family from?"

"Same place I'm from, Tony," Marvin pointedly said.

"Oh! Right, got it." Tony winked at Reima. "Well, I'll let you get back to your dinner. It was nice to meet you all, and, Marv, don't be such a stranger, eh?" Tony clapped Marvin on the back and walked away.

"He knows I hate being called Marv," muttered Marvin.

"What was that all about?" asked Marcia. The waiter arrived before anyone could answer.

The waiter took their drink orders and walked away. Marvin answered Marcia's question.

"I'm a changeling," he quietly said. "A faerie child left in the place of a human one."

The girls both looked confused.

"I'll explain later," said Reima. "This place is too crowded to talk about things like that."

Aubree nodded and picked up her menu.

"But how did he—" began Marcia.

"I told him," said Reima. "Before Aubree's party."

He caught Marcia's eye, trying to silently communicate his full meaning. *All I told him was that you girls are fae. He doesn't know the whole story.*

"Ah." Marcia simply nodded.

Reima expected her to make a bigger deal out of it, especially after how she reacted at his apartment when Ariana told them everything.

Reima opened his menu and winced at the prices.

"I can't decide what I want." Aubree's eyes scanned the menu. "Everything's expensive."

Reima gently touched Aubree's arm. "Don't worry about that. Just order what you what. It's a date, remember? That means I'm paying for you."

"I know, but still."

"Don't worry about it," insisted Reima.

"We'll get a discount, anyway," added Marvin.

Aubree smiled. "Okay. Thank you." She looked back at her menu.

Reima may have given Aubree permission to order whatever she wanted, but that did not mean he could. Aubree ordered plain, alfredo linguini, one of the cheaper menu options. Reima quietly sighed in relief.

"I'll have an eight-ounce rib-eye with a loaded baked potato." He handed the menu back to the waiter.

To Aubree's surprise, Marcia did not dominate the dinner conversation. She spoke more than the rest, but allowed Aubree, Reima, and Marvin to participate. Aubree wanted to know more about Marvin. She wondered about changelings, wanted to ask about them, but Reima was right. They did not know who might be listening in the crowded restaurant. She glanced around the large dining room. All the customers focused on their own tables. No one payed the couples the slightest bit of attention, except for a strange man standing beside the kitchen doors. He seemed to stare right at Aubree. She tapped Reima's arm to get his attention, but when she looked back up, the man had vanished.

"What's wrong?" asked Reima.

Aubree shook her head. "Nothing." *I must have imagined him,* thought Aubree. *Ariana's story has me on edge, that's all.*

"So, what, exactly, is a changeling?" asked Marcia once they were back in Marvin's car after dinner.

"Some faeries, for one reason or another, want a human child to raise," began Marvin. "Most of the time, they simply take a baby from its bed and leave. Sometimes, however, they leave a faerie baby in place of the human one. That faerie baby is raised by human parents who are none the wiser."

"That's what happened to you?" asked Marcia.

Marvin nodded.

"How did you know you were a faerie?" asked Aubree.

"The trees told me."

Aubree looked at Reima for more explanation.

"Marvin is a Willow-man," said Reima. "A male dryad that is connected to a willow tree. Dryads can't be too far away from their trees or they will grow weak and fade away."

Marcia sighed. "I get that, but he said the trees 'told' him. You don't mean literally, do you?"

Marvin nodded again.

"Going through the Veil hides most of our faerie abilities, for example, I can't change into a wolf here, but there are some things that are simply a part of us," Reima explained. "Our senses can be dampened, but not completely hidden. You two wouldn't know because you don't have anything to compare too, but have you ever heard something that no one around could hear, or hear something before the rest of your friends?"

Marcia tilted her head in thought. "Now that you mention it, yeah. I just thought my hearing was better than everyone else's."

Reima nodded. "It is. Elves can see and hear things on a different scale than humans."

"That still doesn't explain how he can talk to trees."

"Doesn't it?" asked Aubree. "He's a dryad. It makes sense that he would be able to talk to trees."

"Yeah, that makes about as much sense as Reima being able to talk to dogs because he's a wolf." Marcia started to laugh, but fell silent when she noticed that no one else laughed with her. "Wait. Can Reima really talk to dogs?"

Reima shook his head. "Not exactly. Dogs don't have an actual language like sentient beings have, but I can sense their needs and wants."

"Seriously?" asked Aubree. Reima nodded. "Cool."

"We got off topic," said Marcia. "We were talking about Marvin."

"Right, sorry."

"Your family is human," Marcia said to Marvin. He nodded in agreement. "Then how did they find out about you being a faerie?"

"I told them. They are my family."

"How did they take it?" asked Aubree, remembering how Marcia freaked when she found out what she was.

"My parents didn't believe me," said Marvin, "but Tony did. Mom and Dad actually scheduled me appointments with several psychiatric doctors because of how strongly I held to my 'delusion' and that I claimed to be able to communicate with trees. Eventually I let it go. There was no way to prove anything and I was tired of being called crazy. I stopped talking about it in front of them. None of that stopped Tony from trying to convince them, though. I think he's still trying."

They continued the discussion until they arrived at Aubree's house. Elliot waited, holding the door, and waved to them as they pulled into the driveway. Marvin got out first in order to open the girls' doors and walk them to the house. Aubree and Reima walked several paces behind the other couple for a moment of privacy.

"Thank you," said Aubree. "I had a great time."

Reima smiled. "I'm glad. I did too."

Aubree took Reima's hand. "That was my first date, you know. Not just with you, but ever. I mean, I know we had the picnic thing a couple months ago, but..."

"Yeah. It—it was mine too," admitted Reima.

"Your what?"

"My first date. Ever."

Aubree stopped walking. "Really?"

Reima nodded.

"But you're gorgeous! How am I the first girl to ever like you?" asked Aubree.

"Actually, you're not," laughed Reima. "You're just the first girl I've ever liked back."

"Really?" Aubree blushed.

"Really."

His eyes locked onto hers. She easily saw the wolf in him—now that she knew the truth. Her gaze moved downward to his mouth and she leaned closer to him. He leaned forward. Aubree's heart pounded. Their lips closed; inches apart. His hot breath sweet on her face.

This is it.

"Hey! Are you two going to stay out there all night?" Marcia's voice floated down to them from the door, breaking the moment. Reima and Aubree quickly pulled away and looked towards the house. Marcia's eyes widened. "Oops...sorry."

Reima took Aubree's hand and walked her to the house.

"Sorry," whispered Marcia again.

Aubree touched her arm to let her know that it was okay.

"Did you guys have fun?" asked Ariana, carrying bowls to the kitchen.

Aubree nodded. "I had a great time."

Winston ran from the hallway and jumped on Aubree, welcoming her home.

"Me, too," said Marcia. "We learned a lot about Marvin and his family."

"Oh, really?" Elliot hung his jacket in the front room closet. "Like what?"

Marcia listed the conversation topics on her fingers. "Like, he didn't just work at Traverso's. His brother owns it. And he's really close to his family, but especially to his brother, even though Tony annoys him. Oh! And he's a changeling."

"Is that so?" asked Ariana. "I've heard of that kind of thing happening. What is it like?"

Marvin shrugged. "I always knew I was different. When I found out what I am, it was a relief. I do wonder who my birth parents are, sometimes."

Marcia touched his arm. He smiled down at her.

"I hate to break up this tender moment, but some of us have to work in the morning," said Teegan.

Marvin nodded and hugged Marcia goodbye, and then said goodbye to Aubree, Ariana, and Elliot.

"Bye, Reima," said Aubree. "I'll see you tomorrow."

Reima hugged Aubree goodbye. "See you tomorrow."

Aubree hoped for another try at a kiss. *Ariana and Elliot are watching, though. I want our first one to be special.*

Reima released her and followed Teegan and Marvin out of the house. Aubree and Marcia lingered in the doorway. They watched the car pull out of the driveway. Marcia blew a kiss after the receding tail-lights.

Elliot stepped up behind the girls. "All right, time to close the door. You're letting bugs inside."

The girls reluctantly stepped inside the house and closed the door.

"I'm glad you girls had fun." Ariana wrapped both girls in a hug. She kissed them on top of the head. "Good night. I love you."

"I love you, too, Ana."

Ariana released the girls and joined Elliot in their bedroom.

Marcia turned to Aubree. "I call first use in the bathroom."

Aubree nodded. "Go ahead."

She went into her room and changed into her pajamas. She stared into her mirror and brushed out the braid in her hair. She paused, remembering the strange guy at the restaurant. *Something about him seemed off somehow. Maybe I should tell Ariana.*

Marcia walked into the room. "Bathroom's all yours."

"Thanks." Aubree stepped into the hall.

She glanced at Ariana and Elliot's closed bedroom door. No light shined from underneath.

She's in bed already, thought Aubree. *That's okay. It was probably my imagination anyway. I don't want to worry her for nothing.*

She continued to the bathroom and washed her face and brushed her teeth. She went back to her room and carefully stepped around Marcia asleep on the roll-away bed. She crawled into her bed and turned off the lamp. Winston jumped up beside her and snuggled under her arm.

"How did Reima know that we were faeries before we knew?" asked Marcia.

Aubree jumped at the sound of her voice. "I thought you were asleep."

"You were gone for less than five minutes," said Marcia. "Who falls asleep that fast?"

"Ariana."

"That's weird."

"What were you saying about Reima?" asked Aubree.

"I was just thinking, he said that he told Marvin that you and I were faeries before your birthday party. We didn't even know until after."

"Ariana told him, I think," yawned Aubree. "She and Elliot both wanted to talk to him in private before I was allowed to hang out with him."

"Oh, okay."

Marcia quieted. Aubree closed her eyes.

"Good night, Aubree," said Marcia.

"Good night, Marcia."

"Sorry again for ruining your first kiss."

"It's okay," said Aubree. "We'll have another chance, eventually."

"Good. I'm glad." Aubree heard Marcia roll over. "Hey, Aubree? What do you think about Marvin?"

"He seems like a good match for you." Aubree's voice sounded far away.

"Yeah, he does. I really like him."

"Good for you."

"What about you and Reima? Do you love him?"

"Marcia, we've only been on one date."

"So? You're a faerie princess. Princesses usually fall in love instantly."

"That's just in stories."

"But our life is like a story right now."

Aubree rolled over and faced the edge of her bed.

"Marcia, I am too tired to talk about this. I like Reima. That's all I know right now. Now, please, let me go to sleep."

"Sorry," whispered Marcia. "Good night."

"Good night."

"I think I might love Marvin."

Aubree hummed in response, too tired for words. She waited for Marica to speak again, but only heard silence. Aubree rolled back over, pulled Winston close, and closed her eyes.

Do I love Reima?

Hidden Identity

15

Ariana sat at the dining room table, peeling potatoes for dinner. A week and a half passed since Claudette went to update the king and queen, and Ariana anxiously awaited any news from home, no matter how small. There was no way of knowing when Claudette would return, or even if King Alberic would consider it safe for her to return at all. Ariana could only imagine the conversation. She thought back to a previous conversation with Teegan.

Teegan and Ariana sat across from each other at Teegan's dining room table. Teegan bit her bottom lip, hands clasped in front of her, eyes downcast.

"This – this is not easy for me to say, but I think you should know why I was banished. It wasn't because of some rebellious, but heroic reaction like Reima." Teegan took a deep breath and looked up at Eirian. "I used to work for Tola. That's how I recognized her spy."

Ariana gasped. She covered her mouth with one hand.

"It was over four centuries ago. I was young and stupid. I learned my lesson." Teegan unclasped her hands. She moved one hand toward Ariana, but stopped short of touching her arm. Ariana nodded for her to continue. "I was small, as a teenager, and Tola promised to help me grow, to get stronger. All she wanted in return was a golden statue from Father's treasure hoard. Easy enough, I thought, but I got caught. Your father banished me himself. Once in the Mortal Realm, I realized my mistake and cut ties. I just thought you should know the truth."

Ariana silently contemplated Teegan's story. She looked into Teegan's eyes and saw sincerity.

Ariana nodded. "I believe you. Thank you for telling me."

Teegan sighed and leaned back in her chair. She smiled at Ariana. "I was afraid I might lose my newest best friend."

Ariana smiled and reached across the table to gently squeeze Teegan's hand. "My father might be suspicious of you, but I trust you. If you hadn't made that mistake four hundred years ago, you wouldn't have recognized the spy. Good things can come out of bad situations. And, for the record, you're my newest best friend, too."

A knock at the door brought Ariana back to the present. She left the peeled potatoes in a bowl of water and walked to the door. She looked through the peephole and grinned.

Ariana quickly unlocked the door and pulled it open. "Claudette!" Ariana, hugged her friend. "You're back!

Come in." She stood aside to allow Claudette to enter. "How was your trip?"

Ariana eagerly watched the other elf walk into the house. Claudette looked refreshed from her time in the Faerie Realm. She held herself straighter, had a new sparkle in her eye, despite the circumstances.

Claudette turned to Ariana. "Eventful. Your parents send their love."

Tears filled Ariana's eyes. "Then they're okay? Tola hasn't harmed them?"

"They are both whole and healthy." Claudette put a reassuring hand on Ariana's shoulder. "However, the events of the past years are very evident in their eyes. They miss you."

"I miss them, too." A tear slid down Ariana's cheek. She wiped her eyes dry before turning back to the potatoes. "I want to hear everything, but the girls are still in school and Elliot's at work. I think we should wait until they get back."

"I agree," said Claudette, "but I don't want you holding a knife right know, you're too excited. How about you wash, and I'll cut."

Ariana smiled and handed the knife over.

Ariana called Teegan and casually invited her and Reima over for dinner. They knew about Tola and deserved to know what Claudette had to say as much as the others. They agreed.

Elliot got home first. "Claudette, you're back." He entered the kitchen.

Ariana hugged Elliot and kissed him.

"She got here about two hours ago," said Ariana. "I haven't heard much. We were waiting for everyone, it saves her from having to repeat herself."

"Sounds good. I'm going to grab a shower before dinner."

Elliot walked off just as the door opened a second time.

"Reima and Teegan said they'd be here soon," said Aubree as she and Marcia came through the door. "They just have to close up."

"Mom!" Marcia dropped her backpack on the floor and ran to hug her mother. "I didn't know you were back!"

"I got back a couple of hours ago." Claudette tightly returned her daughter's embrace. "I wanted to surprise you."

"Well, I have a couple of surprises of my own." Claudette pulled away from Marcia, a look of fear crossing her face. "No! It's nothing to be worried about," Marcia quickly said. "Aubree got me to believe everything. I even kind of remember the palace and Dad a little bit—I think."

Claudette sighed in relief and pulled Marcia close again. "That is wonderful."

"Also, I have a boyfriend. Reima's friend Marvin. Remember him? You met him at Aubree's birthday party."

Claudette nodded. "I think so. He's the boy you've been texting, right?"

Marcia nodded.

"Is this the reason you invited Reima and Teegan over?" asked Aubree. "Because Aunt Claudette is home?"

"Yes, it is," nodded Ariana. "I wanted the whole gang together to hear the report from home."

"Did you remember to call Aunt Charity?" asked Marcia.

"Of course, I called Charity," said Claudette. "She's on her way."

Ariana put the last of the dinner bowls into the sink and joined the others in the living room. Charity sat in Elliot's recliner. Elliot, Ariana, Reima, and Claudette sat on the couch. Aubree sat on the floor in front of Reima, leaning against his legs. Marcia sat in front of her mother. Teegan stood, arms crossed, beside the couch. All attention focused on Claudette as she gave her report.

"Tola is still in Faerie," began Claudette. The group breathed a collective sigh of relief. "Devin and the other guards have been keeping an eye on her for the past ten years. That's the good news. Unfortunately, King Alberic has been unable to arrange an alternate deal. He said that Tola is insistent upon taking Aubree."

"She won't take anything else?" Ariana frowned in disappointment.

Claudette shook her head. "Your parents have offered her gold, jewels, land, anything they can think of. She refused it all, saying they either hand over Aubree, or she'll go back on her end of the deal and take away Ariana's health."

Ariana gasped and Elliot wrapped his arm tighter around her.

"Then why hasn't she done it already?" asked Elliot.

"Because she still doesn't know where you are," said Teegan. "Her magic is limited to the people she can see in her mirrors and spells. If she doesn't know where you are, she can't watch you. That's why she sent out the spies."

"You seem to know a lot about her." Marcia suspiciously eyed Teegan.

"Marcia, you let the adults handle Teegan," said Claudette. "We have already had this discussion with her."

"What did Daddy say we should do?" asked Ariana, bringing the conversation back to the topic at hand.

"He said to sit tight for now," said Claudette. "You're safe, as long as Tola doesn't figure out where you are."

Ariana shook her head. "But I'm tired of hiding. If Daddy and his men know where Tola is, why don't they do something? Not try to make another deal with her, but stop her?"

"Tola is too powerful."

"He's too scared, you mean." Ariana stood up from the sofa and stalked across the room. She stared out the window.

"Ariana," began Aubree.

Ariana spun around. "It has been sixteen years!" she yelled, tears streaming down her face. "We have been here, hiding, waiting for him to do something, anything, for *sixteen* years! And he has done *nothing!*" She paced around the room.

"Ariana, please keep your voice down," warned Claudette.

"I am tired of being called Ariana! I want to be called by my true name again!"

"You know why we can't do that," Elliot quietly said, hoping to calm her.

"Why not? We talk about home, here. You and I speak Elvish here. Why can I not be called by my real name in the privacy of my own home?"

"Ariana," Claudette began. Ariana glared at her. "Eirian," she amended, "your father has not been idle these past years."

"No, he has been watching her," countered Eirian, "trying to make another deal with her. It is not as if that is what started this whole thing."

"He has been doing much more than that," said Claudette, the gentle tone gone from her voice. "He has been researching her, trying to find out where she gets her power. He has sent men all over the realm, into other kingdoms, and chasing even the tiniest whisper of rumor. He and your mother have spent days on end shut up in the library, looking for any scrap of information they could get their hands on. He has even tried to gain audience with the High Queen."

Eirian stopped pacing.

"You were right, Eirian," said Claudette. "He is afraid. He is afraid of losing you, and Aubree, for good. He is afraid of making a rash move and endangering you further." Claudette took Eirian's hands and looked her in the eye. "Your father wants you both at home as much as you do, more, I dare say, but right now, it is still too dangerous. The moment Tola makes any indication that she has figured out where you are hiding, he and his men will move. They will cut her off before she gets a chance to harm you, even if it means putting himself in danger. The information Teegan gave him will also help tremendously."

Eirian looked at Teegan. "What information?"

"Just some stuff I learned during my short time working for her," shrugged Teegan. "Stuff I had kept to myself, thinking I could use it against her if she ever tried to contact me for breach of contract. I figured your father would make better use of it."

"Thank you, Teegan," smiled Eirian, hugging her friend. "That means so much to–"

"Did you hear that?" Reima suddenly asked.

He tilted his head to one side. Everyone stayed quiet and listened.

"Someone's outside," said Teegan after a moment. She jumped up and ran to the window.

Eirian collapsed back onto the couch and pulled Aubree to her. Elior wrapped his arms around them both.

Teegan stared out the window. "You guys wait five minutes, and then get to our apartment," she ordered, without turning around. "Reima, take them the back way. I'm going to go after our new friend and see how much of that he heard."

"Someone should warn the king," said Claudette.

Teegan shook her head and made her way to the door. "Not yet. We don't know who this guy is. It could have just been some random creeper. Get to my apartment and wait for me."

"Thank you, Teegan," said Eirian.

Teegan smiled out of one corner of her mouth. "What are friends for?" she asked before going out into the night.

Hidden Identity

16

Aubree curled up on the sofa in Reima's apartment, and leaned against him. Eirian and Elior sat together on the other side of the couch. Eirian absently stared at the opposite wall, unmoving, eyes distant. Elior held her and stroked her hair. Marcia curled up in her mother's lap in an armchair. Charity stood against one wall, eyes closed, listening for anything from outside. No one made a sound.

They followed Teegan's orders and stealthily made their way to Teegan and Reima's apartment. Three hours passed in silence, waiting on any word from Teegan. Aubree wanted to bring Winston with them, but Eirian made her leave him behind. They did not want the puppy to give them away.

"What's taking her so long?" asked Marcia, her voice loud in the silent room.

"Teegan is a pretty good spy, herself," said Reima. "She probably went to spy on Tola's spies and see how much they know."

"Well, can't you text her or call her or something?"

Claudette shook her head. "No. If her phone went off now, she could get caught."

"Well, we can't just sit here," said Aubree. "What if something happened to her? Shouldn't she have at least tried to get in touch with us by now?"

Reima turned to Aubree. "I've known Teegan a long time. She knows how to take care of herself."

"But what about us?" insisted Aubree. "How long are we supposed to wait here?"

"I think Eirian should decide that," said Charity.

Eirian slowly looked up. She spoke in a far-away voice. "Why me?"

"You are the future queen," said Claudette, "and like it or not, you are the highest authority in this room. Up until now you have been following orders. First the king's, then mine, and now you are letting an exile tell you what to do." Eirian opened her mouth to defend herself, but Claudette put up a hand. "I know she's your friend and I know that she's helping us, and I thank her for that. But right now, you need to step up. You were the one complaining that you were tired of hiding. Well, there is a good chance we have all been discovered, so now I ask. Princess Eirian, what should we do?"

Everyone looked at Eirian, waiting.

She looks like she's about to cry, thought Aubree.

Eirian looked around at each person in the room, trying to find her answer on their faces. She closed her eyes, took a deep, steadying breath, and opened her eyes again.

Eirian nodded once. "We will wait for Teegan until morning. If we haven't heard from her by then, we'll call her. If she doesn't answer, then we will go back home."

"But they already know where we live," protested Aubree.

Eirian turned to her.

"That's not the home I was talking about. We will go back to the Faerie Realm, to the palace, tell Daddy what's happened. He'll prepare the guards and we will fight." Eirian's voice trembled and she paused to take a breath before continuing. "I don't care how strong Tola is. She can't possibly take on a kingdom full of soldiers."

Eirian sounded like she was trying to convince herself, as well as everyone else, that she spoke the truth. Aubree was not quite as sure. If her father's soldiers could take on this woman, they would have done so years ago.

"What about Reima?" asked Aubree. "He's an exile. He can't just go back, can he?"

"Normally, no," said Eirian. "However, these are special circumstances. He can come through with us and I will explain everything to Daddy after things calm down. I will see if I can convince Daddy to look over Reima's case. Daddy was not the one to banish Reima, but he can pardon him."

Aubree nodded and leaned closer to Reima. "Thank you."

Eirian smiled in response.

"Now we're just supposed to keep waiting?" asked Marcia. "Wait to see if we hear from Teegan or not?"

"Yes," said Claudette. "That is exactly what we do. In the meantime, why don't you all try to get some sleep. Charity and I will stay up and wake you if we hear anything."

"The girls can sleep in Teegan's room," suggested Reima. "Eirian and Elior can have my bed, and I can sleep on the couch."

"Sounds good," said Elior.

No one made any move to get up.

"Or we could all just stay in here," suggested Aubree. "Safety in numbers, you know?"

"That sounds better," agreed Marcia.

Normally, Aubree would not have fallen asleep next to a boy, but she felt safe with Reima's arms around her. Everyone else was in the same room, and no one told her to move, so she buried her head in Reima's chest, and closed her eyes. Aubree felt she just closed her eyes when someone shook her awake. She opened one eye to see Eirian standing over her, eyes wide and all color drained from her face. Aubree sat up.

"What happened?" She looked around the still dark room.

Elior, Reima, and Marcia stood by the café stairwell door. Aubree shuddered from a sudden chill. She took Eirian's trembling outstretched hand.

"Change of plan." Eirian helped Aubree off the couch. "We're leaving now."

A pit formed in Aubree's stomach. *Something is not right.* Eirian pulled Aubree into an unexpected hug. Eirian tightly held onto to her sister. A sob escaped her lips.

Aubree's blood ran cold. "Did something happen to Teegan?" She pulled back and looked at Eirian. "Where are Aunt Claudette and Aunt Charity?"

"Still no word from Teegan." Reima put a warm, solid hand on Aubree's shoulder. "Eirian sent Claudette and Charity ahead to warn your parents."

"What happened?" Aubree asked again.

"She found us." Eirian did not need to explain how she knew.

Elior led the group downstairs. Eirian opened the door and stopped short. Standing in the darkened café were three hooded figures, silhouetted from behind by the first rays of dawn coming in through the front window.

"Hello, Eirian," said the figure in the center. "I have been searching for you."

Eirian stepped in front of Aubree and Marcia, standing between the girls and Tola. Elior and Reima stood on either side of her. Tola and her minions walked further into the café. There was no way to get around them. Eirian quickly glanced behind her. She could see the staircase that led back up to Teegan and Reima's apartment. They could still get out that way if need be.

"Did you really think you could hide from me forever?" asked Tola. Even speaking English, her familiar, silkily mocking tone sent chills across Eirian's body. "I told you I would find you."

Tola pulled back her hood and Eirian's heart pounded. Teegan was right, Tola had found a way to resist the Veil's glamour. There was no way anyone could mistake Tola for human. The cold eyes and deceivingly charming smile were exactly the same as Eirian remembered. She wore loose black pants and a flowing white blouse instead of a dress. Her crystal comb still glittered in her hair. Eirian struggled to keep her composure as tears pricked at her eyes. She found it hard to breathe. Elior took her hand. She gave him a grateful smile and took a deep breath.

"Now, just give me the girl, and we can all go home," continued Tola with a shrug of one shoulder.

"No." Eirian's voice trembled with anger and fear. "You can't have her."

Tola sighed. "We have been through all of this already. I am in no mood to stand here in this disgusting world discussing a matter that has already been resolved. Now, give me the girl!" Tola reached out for Aubree, and Reima snapped at her arm, missing by centimeters. Tola jerked her arm back.

"Stay away from her," snarled Reima.

"Down, boy," taunted Tola. "I have no business with you."

"If it involves Aubree, then it involves me," said Reima.

"Oh, do not tell me that you are attached already?" Tola pouted, addressing Aubree. "I am sorry, my dear, but I cannot allow you to have any pets. They shed everywhere, the filthy things. Not to mention the flea problem." Tola gave an exaggerated shudder. "Now, come on. I have been patient long enough." Tola held out her hand.

"Surely you aren't expecting us to just hand her over," said Elior.

"That is exactly what I expect, *halfling*." Tola spat out the last word.

Eirian incredulously laughed; a short, sharp sound.

Tola cocked her head to the side, like a bird, and looked at Eirian. "Does that amuse you, Princess?" she asked. "I have been kept waiting for far too long, biding my time while you played hide-and-seek. When your father first approached me after you and Aubree had disappeared, I thought he had come to his senses, that he was ready to give me what he promised me."

Tola looked past Eirian to smirk at Aubree. Eirian moved her head and blocked Aubree from view. Tola glared at her, but continued her speech.

"Imagine my disappointment when, instead of making good on the deal he had already made, he foolishly tried to make another one." Tola sighed as if she were talking about a disobedient child. "He held on to his delusion of getting out of our deal. He would not even tell me where you were."

"How did you find us?" demanded Eirian.

She knew, if she could just keep Tola talking long enough, it would give Charity and Claudette time to get her father, and his army, and bring them to the café.

"I hope you are not trying to stall me, Princess." Tola wagged a finger in front of Eirian's face. Tola's minions chuckled. "It will not do you any good. I locked the gate. No one from Faerie will be able to cross unless I allow it. Of course, your precious nurse-maid and her sister have been allowed to enter Faerie, but your backup is not coming."

Eirian squeezed Elior's hand tighter.

"B-but, that's not possible," stammered Eirian. "Only the High Queen can lock the gate."

"You continue to underestimate me," smirked Tola, "but I see no harm in answering your original question. How did I find you? That was simple. I waited for you to make a mistake."

Eirian thought back to earlier, to the discussion she had at her house, and the man that Teegan had chased down the street.

"Your nurse-maid was not careful enough when she returned from reporting to your father. She did not even notice that she was being followed," chuckled Tola. "But your dragon was the most help."

"What have you done with Teegan?" growled Reima.

Tola made a motion with her hand, and two more of her minions entered, dragging something between them.

Teegan! Eirian froze at the sight of her unconscious friend covered in blood. *Is she breathing? I can't tell. She's too far away.*

Reima growled.

"She was a tough one," said Tola.

Eirian cringed at the word *was*.

"Much stronger than the last time we met," continued Tola. "Not stronger than me, of course. I did eventually get the information I needed out of her, but it took a truth spell and I had to re-attach her tongue after she bit it off trying to resist. Dragons are stubborn creatures. It is a pity, though," Tola glanced over her shoulder as she spoke, "if she had just accepted my offer to return to my service, she would still be alive. Stupid girl."

"Shut up!" snapped Reima. "If you say one more word about her, I swear I will rip out your throat."

"Will you now?" Tola took a step closer to Reima. "That *would* be a surprise. Especially since your dragon failed at the same task."

Reima lunged forward. Eirian held him back. She wanted to hurt Tola too, but it would be suicide to attack her head on. Tola still had her magic. They were practically human. They still needed to protect Aubree.

Tola laughed again and turned her attention to Eirian. "Perhaps the young princess has some sense after all. I will tell you what. I did not make a second deal with the king because he had nothing I want. You, on the other hand, do."

Eirian felt a tiny surge of hope, immediately followed by suspicion.

"What do you want?" asked Eirian.

"I want what I have wanted from the start: a child. Although Aubree is the child I was promised, I will let you keep her, *if*," Tola paused for effect, "you give me your daughter instead."

"Eirian doesn't have a daughter," said Elior in an even tone.

A sly smile spread across Tola's mouth. "Not yet, but she will in a matter of months."

"Wh—what do you mean?" asked Eirian, certain everyone in the room heard her heart pounding.

"Have you not figured that out, yet, Princess?" Tola pressed a hand to Eirian's abdomen.

Eirian gasped and jerked away.

"Don't touch her!" snapped Elior.

"You're lying," said Eirian, her voice barely above a whisper.

"Am I? Was I lying when I told you your mother was pregnant?" Tola paused, waiting for a response. The group remained silent. She continued. "You can either hand over your sister or your daughter, those are your choices. You have until the end of the day to decide." Tola turned and started to walk away. "Just to make sure you do not try to run off again," Tola waved her hand and a cloudy purple barrier appeared in front of the doors and over the windows.

Eirian clasped one hand to her belly. *What can I do?* They could not escape. Tola retained her power. *I will never hand over Aubree or my – baby? Am I really pregnant?* She looked to Elior for help, but her eyes landed on Teegan lying on the floor. Eirian clenched her fists. "No."

Tola stopped walking and sharply cocked her head to one side. "What did you say?" Tola slowly turned around.

"I said no," repeated Eirian, her voice cold as steel. "I am done playing the victim. You cannot have Aubree or my daughter. You have tormented my family long enough. No more." Eirian stepped away from Elior and Reima. She stood face to face with the witch.

"Are you sure you want to do this, Princess?" asked Tola. "If I do not get a child, then your father will have failed to uphold his end of the agreement. If that happens, then I will have to go back on my part. That would leave you very ill, Princess, fatally ill. Is that what you want?"

Eirian shook her head. "No. What I want is for you to rot in a dungeon for all time. That way, you will not hurt anyone else ever again, but I know that will not happen without a fight. Here is what I propose. Fight me. If you win, you can take away my health after my daughter is born, but if I win, then you must turn yourself in. You must tell us the secret of your strength and how to overcome it and agree to be locked up in our strongest cell."

"Eirian, no!" exclaimed Elior.

"Are you crazy?" shouted Reima. "She's too strong. She'll kill you. She's already killed Teegan!"

"What do you say?" asked Eirian without turning around.

Tola raised one eyebrow. "I assume you are expecting a fair fight?"

"No. Because I know you will not agree to a fair fight."

"Smart girl," Tola extended her hand. "You have a deal."

Eirian reached for Tola's hand. Elior and Reima rushed forward to stop her. Tola's minions rushed to stop Elior and Reima.

"No!" Tola waved her other hand and everyone froze in place. "Now, where were we?"

Eirian shook Tola's hand, sealing the deal. A rush of magical wind filled the café. Tola grinned, walked a few feet away, and removed her cloak. Her hair magically wrapped itself atop her head to keep from tripping over it. A sword materialized in each of her hands and she tossed one to Eirian, who clumsily caught it. Tola laughed in triumph.

Eirian ignored her and adjusted the sword to get the best grip. She tried to remember what Elior and Devin taught her about stance.

"Not used to holding a sword, are we, Princess?" taunted Tola.

"At least I don't have to use magic to hide my weakness," Eirian shot back. "I succeed or fail using my own strength."

Hatred flashed across Tola's face. She advanced. Eirian barely raised her sword in defense.

Hidden Identity

17

Aubree knew, from listening to Eirian's story, that Tola was evil, but she was unprepared for the feeling of dread that filled her the moment Tola removed her hood. Tola emanated immense power. Aubree listened to Tola and Eirian go back and forth and wondered what this woman wanted with her, and then, just for a moment, Tola's eyes locked onto hers and she knew. Tola wanted to teach her.

"*You can be like me,*" her eyes said. "*Come with me, and I will give you power beyond your wildest imagination.*"

A vision flashed in Aubree's mind. Aubree sat beside Tola on a glittering black throne. Fae of all species stood before them, waiting for their turn to speak. Aubree raised her head as a pixie approached.

"Please, your Majesties," the pixie pleaded, "my sister has been missing for several weeks now. I fear she is lost. Will you ensure that she is found safely? I will give anything to have her safe."

Foolish girl, thought Aubree. She glanced over at Tola, who nodded in agreement. Aubree stood, silver hair cascading down her shoulders, and pulled a contract out of thin air.

"We will find your sister," promised Aubree. "Sign here."

A silver pen appeared in her other hand. The pixie took the pen and eagerly wrote her name at the bottom, sealing the deal and signing her sister, who would be found safe, as they promised, into Tola's service. Aubree smirked and rolled up the contract.

The sound of metal clashing against metal ended the vision. Aubree blinked; Eirian and Tola engaged in a sword fight. Aubree winced; Eirian seemed to be losing. On the defense, she did fine, blocking Tola's blade with ease. When she moved in for the attack, however, Tola would raise a hand and Eirian's blade would stop an inch from its target. Aubree looked around to see why no one was helping and saw Elior and Reima, as well as Tola's minions, frozen in place. Their eyes moved, but nothing else. Aubree felt them struggling to break free. Marcia huddled in a corner of the storeroom, sobbing, and Teegan laid in front of the café door.

Aubree inched out of the storeroom and slowly slid across the floor to Teegan. She periodically glanced at Tola, hoping the swordfight held the witch's attention. Tola said that Teegan was dead, but Aubree felt a tiny flicker of life buried deep inside her. She shook Teegan's shoulder, but nothing happened. She shook her a little harder, but Teegan still did not respond. Aubree took her wrist and felt for a pulse, like she learned in health class. Nothing. Aubree knew Teegan was not completely dead. She needed a way to reach the spark, maybe Aubree could make it bigger, then Teegan might wake up and help.

She glanced over to where Eirian and Tola fought. Eirian grew tired, her swings lazy and slow. Tola looked fresh, her movements crisp. Aubree needed to do something fast. A glimmer of light caught her eye; something lay on the floor near the counter. Aubree crawled closer, using overturned tables as cover. Tola's crystal comb. Aubree glanced at the evil faerie. *It must have come loose during the fighting.*

A powerful energy emanated from the comb. Aubree reached for it with a trembling hand, the power like pins and needles in her fingers. She picked it up. Aubree's senses instantly grew. She immediately knew where everyone stood. She found them like sonar; their energy filled the room. She felt their thoughts and emotions; Marcia's helplessness, Reima's rage, Elior's hatred toward Tola. Marcia wished to be braver. Reima wanted to tear out Tola's throat. Elior simply wanted to get free and help his wife. Aubree turned her attention to her sister. Eirian feared she would lose the fight, along with everything she tried so hard to protect. A glance at the witch showed Tola's growing boredom of toying with Eirian.

Aubree clutched the comb and crawled back over to Teegan. The flicker of life quickly faded within her. Aubree closed her eyes and took a deep breath. She felt for the spark. A smile creased her lips. She knew what to do to bring Teegan back to life. The spark intensified, growing stronger and stronger. Aubree watched the spark travel through the woman, heading for Teegan's heart.

The comb grew hot. A voice, somewhere in the back of Aubree's mind, told her to drop the comb. Aubree only squeezed it tighter.

I can bring her back, she thought. *I will bring Teegan back, and then I will stop Tola from hurting my sister. I will free Elior and Reima, and show them how strong I can be by destroying Tola. I am stronger than she is. I can rule the entire realm of Faerie.*

Aubree's eyes snapped open. *Where had that last thought come from?* She glanced down at the comb in her hand. It harmlessly glittered in her palm. *Did the idea come from the comb? That's not possible.* She held the comb up to her face for closer inspection. *Where else could the idea have come from?*

The vision of Aubree in power flashed in her mind again. This time, Aubree saw the cost. In order for her to rule the way Tola wanted, Aubree would need to get rid of everyone ahead of her. That meant, not only her parents and the High Queen, but Eirian, Elior, and their unborn child. Her friends would be too afraid to be near her. She would lose Reima. He would stay with her out of love and loyalty, but eventually her love of power would win out over her love of him. He would fade from her life, forgotten and alone.

It is worth it, said the voice in her head.

"No, it's not," said Aubree out loud.

She sucked in a breath and broke the comb in half.

The comb's snap echoed in the room. A sword clattered to the café's tile floor. Elior fell on his face; the spell holding him in place gone. He scrambled to his feet and hurried to Eirian.

Tola lay on the ground in a pool of blood. Eirian knelt beside her, tears streaming down her face. She pressed

Tola's cloak against the wound. The blood flowed freely, unstoppable. Elior put his arm around Eirian and held her close.

"I didn't mean to kill her," muttered Eirian between sobs. "I didn't mean to kill her."

"I know," Elior whispered in her ear.

Reima looked to the storeroom where he had left Aubree and Marcia. He saw Marcia in a corner, tears ran down her face. He did not see Aubree. His heart pounded. He frantically swept his eyes around the room, noting that Tola's minions had disappeared.

There she is. Reima sighed in relief.

Aubree knelt over Teegan's body by the café's entrance. He walked across the floor to her; she did not look up. Reima put one hand on Aubree's shoulder and closed his eyes.

I can't believe Teegan's really gone. Tears filled Reima's eyes. He allowed them flow. He remembered the first time he met Teegan, decades before, how she found him, alone and afraid, wandering the streets after his banishment, and brought him into her home. *She gave me my first job, taught me to speak English and how to survive in the Mortal Realm.* He clenched a fist, sharp fingernails digging crescent marks into his soft palm. *She was my best friend, my partner. She didn't deserve this.* He glanced at Tola's body. *How can Eirian grieve that monster? She killed Teegan! I would have killed her myself!* Reima turned back to Teegan. *No.* He put a hand on her shoulder. *No!* Reima threw back his head and howled, pouring into the sound all his rage, grief, and regret. He leaned back on his knees, spent. *Goodbye, Teegan.*

"I can't believe it," said Aubree in a hushed tone. Reima opened his mouth to agree. "I can't believe I brought her back."

Reima snapped his mouth shut and opened his eyes. Aubree turned to look at him. Her eyes showed a myriad of emotions: fear, sadness, confusion, and amazement.

"What do you mean you brought her back?" asked Reima.

"Look at her." Aubree nodded at Teegan. "She's breathing."

Reima looked down in disbelief. He saw the slow rise and fall of Teegan's chest. He grabbed Teegan's wrist and felt a faint pulse. It grew stronger with each beat of her heart.

Reima laughed in relief. "She's alive. She's really alive."

Eirian, Elior, and Marcia joined them.

"I don't understand," sniffed Eirian. "Tola said she was dead."

"She was," laughed Aubree. "I brought her back."

Teegan coughed interrupting Aubree's explanation. She yanked her hand out of Reima's grasp and started swatting at the air. Her mouth opened in a silent scream. "Get away from me!" croaked Teegan in a dry, raspy voice.

"Teegan, it's okay," said Reima. "You're in the café."

"You're safe," agreed Aubree. "I'm safe. We are all safe."

Teegan stopped trying to hit them and opened her eyes. She stared at the ceiling with blank, unfocused eyes. She slowly locked onto Reima and the others.

"What happened?" she asked, struggling to sit up.

Aubree took her hand and helped her up while Elior got her a glass of water.

"That's what we were wondering," said Reima.

"What's this?" asked Marcia, reaching for something on the floor.

"Don't touch that!" shouted Aubree and Teegan at the same time.

Marcia yelped in surprise and yanked her hand back.

"It's Tola's comb," said Eirian.

"It's also the source of her power," explained Teegan. "Give me a moment." She drank the glass of water from Elior and sat at a nearby table. The others gathered around and she told her story.

"I chased the faerie at the window to a cave hidden in the woods on the far side of the park. No one was around, so I confronted him and asked him about Tola and her plans." She frowned; her throat parched. Elior brought her another glass of water. "I didn't know there was a tear in the Veil at the back of the cave. A second faerie stepped through, saw us, and moved back to get Tola." She offered an embarrassed smile. "Things went downhill from there. Tola captured me, tortured me for information – which I didn't give – then she got angry and stabbed me in the chest. The next thing I remember, I woke up here." Teegan finished her story, leaving out gruesome details of her torture.

Aubree told her side. "I saw a vision. Tola wanted to train me to become like her and rule over Faerie. When I touched the comb, everything became clearer. I could sense you all, where you stood, what you felt—everything. I felt a spark of life in Teegan and used the comb to bring her back."

Marcia creased her brow in confusion. "I don't understand. If you could sense what Tola wanted, why couldn't she sense you and figure out what you were doing?"

"Because she wasn't strong enough," answered Aubree. "That's another reason she wanted me on her side, because she knew that I would be stronger than her."

"Stronger than Tola?" whispered Eirian in amazement.

Aubree nodded. "The cost was too much, though. It would mean I would lose all of you."

Tears filled her eyes and Reima pulled her close.

"What do we do now?" asked Elior.

"I don't know," admitted Eirian. "The gate must still be locked or else Daddy would be here by now."

"You could go through the tear," suggested Teegan. "I can show you where it is and you could go talk to the king. Then, maybe he could send word to the High Queen that the gate has been sealed and she could unlock it."

"That's not a bad idea," said Eirian. "Lead the way."

"Wait, what about Winston?" asked Aubree. "We left him back at home."

"We can go check on him," said Eirian, "but I don't think we should take him with us just yet. We don't know where the tear leads and we may have to travel a long way before we reach the palace." Eirian glanced at Teegan.

Teegan nodded in agreement. "You're probably right. The tear most likely leads to Tola's castle in the middle of the Razor Wood. Not the place for a puppy."

"Razor Wood?" asked Marcia. "What do you mean, Razor Wood?"

Eirian shuddered at the name. "It's where Tola lives—lived. It is a dark forest where the bark on the trees is razor sharp. That's where Tola took me when she spoke to me in my dreams."

"That sounds horrible!" exclaimed Marcia.

Eirian shuddered. "It is not a place I look forward to going back to."

Elior and Aubree each put a hand on her shoulder.

"Don't worry," said Elior. "We will be right there with you the whole time."

Aubree nodded in agreement. Eirian smiled.

"I know. Thank you."

"Are we ready to go?" asked Teegan.

"Should you be walking?" asked Marcia. "I mean, you were dead just a few minutes ago."

"I'm fine," insisted Teegan. "Aubree's magic worked better than she expected, I think. I feel better than I have in a century."

Hidden Identity

18

They left the café and headed for Eirian's house. Aubree checked on Winston and asked their neighbor to watch him for a day or two. Teegan then led them to the hidden cave.

"Wait." Marcia stopped short as they walked through Westin Park. "This is Marvin's tree." She broke away from the group and ran to the base of the large willow tree. She disappeared through the leafy curtain. She reappeared several minutes later with Marvin.

"I told him what happened," said Marcia. "He can come too, right?"

Eirian nodded her head. They followed Teegan to the cave.

"The tear should be somewhere back here." Teegan put her hand against the back wall of the cave.

"I can see it. It's right here." Aubree touched a section of the cave wall. The wall shimmered under her fingers.

"How did you see it?" asked Marcia. "I don't see anything."

Aubree shrugged. "I guess some of Tola's power stayed behind when I broke the comb."

"Just as long as you don't go crazy on us."

"I promise," said Aubree. "I don't think there's enough left over for me to go crazy like that, anyway."

"I expect it will get a little bit stronger on the other side of the Veil," warned Teegan.

"Right, the Veil dampens faerie magic." Aubree took a deep breath. "I think I'll be okay."

"I'm sure you will be," said Reima.

Aubree smiled and blushed.

"Well, are we ready to go?" asked Elior. "Eirian?"

Eirian touched the wall near the tear and felt the strange energies that made up the Veil; slick and smooth under her fingers, like a sturdy, satin-covered bubble. She slid her hand around the wall until she found the tear, a five-foot-long slash, only wide enough for one person at a time to cross.

"Be careful over there," said Teegan. "Send us word as soon as you can."

Eirian rubbed the edges of the tear between her fingers. She looked around at the others. Marcia had tears in her eyes again, most likely from fear of what they would find on the other side. Marvin stroked her hair with one hand and whispered something in her ear. Elior waited, eager to finally go back home. Teegan stood, arms folded across her chest, distancing herself from the others. Reima and Aubree held each other tight, reminding Eirian of the night she thought she had to say goodbye to Elior.

Eirian firmly shook her head. "No."

"What do you mean no?" asked Teegan.

"I mean, you are coming with us," said Eirian.

Teegan rolled her eyes. "We can't. Banished, remember. That means forever. Reima and I can't go back to Faerie."

"I'm next in line to be queen," countered Eirian. "You can come if I say you can come."

"But you're not queen yet," insisted Teegan. "So, it's still illegal."

"Look, we have no idea what is on the other side of that tear," Eirian pointed out, "but you said yourself that it most likely leads to Tola's wood. You are the only one who has been there, awake that is, and therefore, you know the way back. Besides, if we do run into trouble, I would rather have a wolf and a dragon with us. I will deal with my father later. He's already going to be angry with me for going behind his back and marrying Elior."

"What is he going to say about Reima?" asked Aubree.

"I'll talk to him about that, too," promised Eirian. "There's really no point in worrying about that right this moment. We still have to get to the palace."

"Right," said Reima. "Everything will be okay."

Teegan relented. "Alright, we'll go, but I'd better not get blamed for this."

"Thank you, Teegan." Eirian smiled and hugged her friend, then she went back to the Veil. "Is everyone ready? Then let's go." She took a deep breath and stepped through the tear in the Veil, back into her own world.

Her senses instantly sharpened. The clean, fresh air of the Faerie Realm filled her lungs and made her lightheaded after sixteen years in the Mortal Realm. She lifted a hand and saw, once again, clear, snow-white skin. She wiggled her long, slender fingers and then reached up to touch the dearly missed point of her ears. She smiled in relief and turned to watch the others. Elior came through next. His face showing the same relief and joy that she felt about being back in her own skin. Marcia was next, followed by Marvin, then Aubree and Reima.

Aubree let out a small yelp as she saw Reima. He looked much the same, other than the gray wolf ears that poked out from his hair and his tail. Aubree giggled as Reima experimentally wagged his tail.

"It's been a long time since I've had this," he said.

"I think it's cute." Aubree reached over and scratched him behind the ears.

Reima leaned into the touch.

"Oh!" exclaimed Marcia.

"What is it?" asked Aubree, pausing her motion.

"You're taller than Reima," said Marcia. "I thought he was taller."

"You're taller, too, Marcia," said Eirian. "You're as tall as Marvin, now. Look."

Marcia turned and held her hand up to her forehead, moving it slowly across the gap between them, to touch Marvin in the same place.

"It's part of being an Elf," explained Eirian.

"At least you don't have leaves for hair." Marvin lifted a rough, bark-skinned hand and tucked a long strand of bright green, willow-leaf hair behind a pointed ear. "I've never actually seen what I look like in my true form."

Marcia kissed Marvin on the tip of his branch-like nose. "You may be covered in bark, but you still look adorable, like a walking tree."

Eirian smiled at the couple and turned back to the tear in the Veil.

"Where's Teegan?" she wondered aloud. "I hope she didn't change her mind."

Elior nodded toward the tear. "No, here she comes."

Teegan changed the most. She looked mostly human, as did all animal fae until they transformed, but talons replaced her toes. Her fingers ended in wickedly sharp claws, and a long, sinuous black tail trailed behind her. The biggest difference, however, was the enormous set of wings folded against her back. Eirian knew, from conversations with Teegan, that her wings could reach a span of eight feet across, when stretched out, and that was before she took on the form that most people think of when they picture a dragon.

"Wow," said Marcia.

Aubree stared at Teegan with wide eyes.

"You done staring?" Teegan asked, rolling her eyes. "We need to get out of here before someone sees us."

"Where, exactly, is 'here'?" asked Reima.

Eirian looked around. They stood in a courtyard, similar to the one in her parents' palace, but made of shiny, black stones rather than white. Veins of deep purple spread through the stone. A very large pool sat on one side of the courtyard, against a harsh dark palace comprised of jagged edges and sharp angles.

The trees of the Razor Wood closely surrounded the courtyard on the remaining three sides. Seeing it again brought back memories of Eirian's last visit; she shuddered. She felt a hand on her back and turned her head to see Elior. He did not say anything; just pulled her closer and planted a kiss on her cheek.

"Um, guys," said Aubree, "I think we have company."

Eirian turned and noted Aubree was right. A group of fae approached and more watched from the various windows and doorways of the dark palace. Eyes peered in through the woods. She recognized a couple of the faeries, Tola's café henchmen.

"There she is," said one, a faun with a broken horn and matted gray fur.

"That's the one who killed the mistress," said the other, a blue-skinned goblin.

Both spoke Common and pointed directly at Eirian. She looked around at the group surrounding them. Tola's minions far outnumbered their own group of seven. Most of them did not appear very smart. Their diminished intelligence gave her an idea.

Eirian squared her shoulders and stepped in front of her friends to address the crowd.

"Yes, I did kill Tola," she said in a strong, clear voice. "I am Princess Eirian of the Kingdom of Varia. Your mistress, Tola, has been defeated. There is no longer any need for you to remain here. I understand that many of you were only serving Tola to pay off a deal you made with her. Come with me, to my castle, and I can guarantee you a fair trial."

Eirian held her breath and waited for a response. The fae around her blinked and murmured to each other. For a moment, Eirian believed they might actually listen to her. A troll slowly raised his hand.

"If we go with you, we won't get in trouble?" he asked.

"That's not what she said." A green-skinned rusalka – an aquatic faerie created from the spirit of a drowned woman – sat on the edge of the pool. She rolled white, pupil-less eyes at the troll. "She said we'd get a fair trial."

"Whasat mean?" asked the troll.

A fox faerie sighed. "It means we would still be punished, but the king and queen would 'discuss' it first."

The troll scratched his head.

"What Mistress think?" asked the troll.

"The mistress is dead," sneered the faun, gesturing towards Eirian. "Our princess killed her."

"Were you not listening or did you just forget already?" The rusalka tossed her moldy black hair over one shoulder in annoyance.

"Uh...both?"

"Well I don't think it matters much," said the goblin. "She's only the princess. She can't guarantee us a fair trial."

"Yes, I can," insisted Eirian, struggling to be heard over the muttering of the crowd. "My father will listen to me. He—"

A deep booming voice cut her off. "Why are you even discussing this? She killed the mistress! This is probably a trick to kill us too."

"He's right!" shouted another voice. "What has royalty ever done for us, anyway?"

Eirian tried again to get control of the crowd, but it was too late. She did not know what to do. There were too many to fight, and if they tried to run for the Wood, they would be too quickly overrun. Out of the corner of her eye, she saw Teegan growing and transforming.

Hidden Identity

19

Aubree emerged from the cave and found herself in the courtyard of a terrifying black stone palace.

"Oh!" She realized what the others meant when they said the Veil dampened her natural faerie senses. Everything was crisp and clear. Aubree heard the wind blow through the leaves of the black forest that surrounded them. Her magical ability strengthened too. Energy flowed through her veins, not quite as strong when she touched the comb, but enough to make her uncomfortable.

She tried to ignore the evil vibe of the palace and the surrounding area by focusing on her friends. Her sister stood taller, as did Elior. Reima sprouted wolf ears and a tail. She did not notice the physical changes in herself, namely her height, until Marcia pointed it out.

Aubree sensed the group of fae around them before she saw them.

"Um, guys," she said, speaking mainly to Eirian and Elior. "I think we have company."

Aubree had never seen anything stranger than the collection of creatures in front of her. Some of them she could name, like the faun and the goblin that stood in front of the crowd. There were trolls and elves and pixies and giants. Several of the faeries looked more like Reima, mostly human, but with various animal parts:

ears, tails, eyes, and such. Aubree saw several that she did not know, like the corpse-like girl with pale, sunken eyes sitting on the edge of the pool.

Aubree watched and listened as Eirian appealed to the crowd. No one spoke English, but Aubree somehow understood them. Aubree smiled, proud of her sister's speech.

She really sounds like a ruler. If I grew up in the palace, as a princess, would I be able to speak like that?

Voices of dissent peppered the crowd. Eirian's voice faltered.

Maybe I can say something to help get them back under control?

Teegan sensed her motives and held her back. "There's nothing that you could say that would calm them now. I have an idea." Teegan grew larger and larger, her clothes ripping free. She dropped onto all fours. Everyone around made room for her as her arms, legs, neck, and tail lengthened and thickened. Her wings, already huge, grew even bigger. Her skin hardened into shiny black scales. The transformation complete, she stretched her neck and roared, releasing a jet of flame into the air.

Tola's faeries shrank back.

Quickly, climb on! Teegan spoke inside Aubree's head rather than out loud. Teegan laid down on the ground, but still towered above the group.

Aubree wondered how to get up onto Teegan's back. Elior touched her shoulder.

"Just jump," he told her. "Let your instincts take over. Watch."

Elior effortlessly leaped the distance from the ground to Teegan's spiked back. Eirian jumped next, gently landing behind Elior.

Aubree took a deep breath. "I can do this," she whispered. "Just let my instincts take over."

She looked up and saw where she needed to land, took a few steps back, and jumped.

"That was awesome!" she laughed as she landed behind Eirian.

The only one who needed help getting on was Marvin. He jumped with his arms raised. Eirian and Elior caught hold of his hands and pulled him the rest of the way up.

Everyone on? asked Teegan. *Then hold on tight. I'm taking off.*

Spikes covered Teegan's back; handholds for her passengers. Aubree wrapped her arms around the nearest spike as Teegan pushed off into the air. Tola's faeries recovered from their initial shock and surged forward. Aubree did not dare to look, but she heard the grumbling and shouts of frustration below her.

"We made it!" Marcia shouted from behind her.

We're not out of the woods yet, said Teegan. *There's still a long way to go before we reach the king's castle.*

A roar pierced the air behind them. Aubree wanted to put her hands over her ears, to block out the deafening sound, but she did not dare let go of the spike.

Teegan looked behind them. *This is not good.*

"What is it?" asked Eirian.

Another dragon. Teegan sped up.

Aubree twisted her body to see behind her without losing her grip. A dragon with bright red scales chased them. It looked about the same size as Teegan and coming up fast. The dragon opened its mouth and a jet of flame shot out. Teegan swerved to avoid it. Aubree instinctively ducked. The heat washed over her, dispelling the chill of the air rushing past.

Give up, traitor! shouted the other dragon, speaking the same, strange language as Tola's faeries.

Aubree recognized his voice as the one that first spoke against Eirian in the crowd.

You're the traitor! Teegan shouted back in the same language. *Tola was evil! The world is better off without her! Both worlds!*

The other dragon roared again, much closer than last time, and snapped at Teegan. Teegan swerved again. Aubree nearly lost her grip. Marcia shrieked.

"I've got you," said Marvin.

He's gaining, said Teegan, *and I can't fight him with you guys on my back.*

"Can you get low enough to drop us off?" asked Eirian, shouting over the rushing winds.

I think so, said Teegan. *I can see a clearing ahead that looks big enough for me.*

"Eirian, are you sure?" asked Elior. "That's the Razor Wood beneath us."

"I know that," said Eirian. "Just do it."

Alright. Hold on!

Teegan folded her wings and shot toward the trees, aiming for the clearing. The ground rushed up at them. Aubree's stomach flipped at the sudden descent. The wind tore at her clothes. Her grip on the spike slipped. The other dragon followed close behind.

Don't drop me. Don't drop me. The phrase repeated itself in Aubree's mind. She kept her eyes open, despite every instinct to close them.

Teegan spread her wings, stopping her descent. Aubree smashed into her rough, scaly hide. The other dragon shot past in a red blur. *Now!* shouted Teegan.

Aubree let go of the spike and fell to the ground. She hit the ground, absorbed the shock with her knees, and rolled a few feet. A roar echoed above her, and she looked up. The other dragon had already come back around and clamped his jaws onto one of Teegan's wings. Teegan roared in pain. Boiling hot dragon blood rained down. Aubree yelped and jumped out of the way.

The red dragon released Teegan. Her injured wing hung in tatters. Teegan flapped her remaining wing hard and fast, staying aloft. The dragon moved in for another attack. Teegan was ready for him. She lunged and bit his neck. He spun to throw her off but Teegan held on. She folded her wings, putting her entire weight on the other dragon's neck. The two locked in combat, spinning and twisting. The red dragon snapped once more at Teegan. Exhaustion took its toll and the red dragon stopped struggling. His wings and tail hung limp. Teegan released him. The dead dragon crashed somewhere in the forest.

Teegan opened her good wing again and slowly circled down. She landed and transformed, shrinking down until she was once again Teegan sized.

"You're naked!" exclaimed Marcia, clapping one hand over Marvin's eyes.

"Usually, I would have taken my clothes off before I transformed, so I'd have something to put back on." Teegan winced as she spoke. "This was an emergency."

"We'll think about clothes later," said Eirian. "Right now, we need to look at that wing."

Aubree helped Eirian stretch out Teegan's torn wing.

"That looks really bad." Marcia still held her hand over Marvin's eyes.

Teegan's wing resembled a kite whose body had torn away from its frame. Blood seeped from the wound, puddling on the ground.

"We need something to stop the bleeding," said Reima.

Eirian shook her head. "What we need is a healer. The skin has to be put back in just the right way or else Teegan will never fly again."

"We don't have a healer," said Elior.

Aubree stepped up. "Maybe we do. I can still feel some of Tola's power. It's not much, but it may be enough to fix Teegan's wing."

"No," said Teegan, through gritted teeth. "It's too dangerous."

"I have to try."

"Look, I'm never going to fly again, anyway," snapped Teegan. "Once we get you guys home, I'm going back to the Mortal Realm. The only reason I came here in the first place was because Eirian asked me to."

"We still need to stop the bleeding," insisted Eirian.

Teegan looked at her wing. "The dead skin needs to be cut away. Otherwise it will keep pulling and I'll start bleeding again."

"How do we do that?" asked Marcia, turning Marvin around so his back was to the group. "This is just a guess, but I don't suppose there many things that can cut through dragon skin."

"The bark on the trees can cut through anything." Eirian pointed to the forest. "Unfortunately, that means that it will also cut through the skin on our hands if we tried to hold it."

"I can do it," offered Reima. "My skin is thicker than an Elf's."

"It's not thicker than dragon skin," Aubree pointed out.

"I'll wrap the bark in a strip of cloth first," said Reima. "It's not the best protection, but it's the best we've got. Then, I can use the cloth to wrap up my hand if I do get cut."

Elior turned to Aubree. "It's better than doing nothing."

Eirian touched her cheek, remembering the wound Tola gave her all those years ago. "The sap of the trees is poisonous. See if you can find some bark that has fallen off the tree."

"Here's a piece." Marvin held a piece of black bark between two fingers, careful not to touch the sharp edges.

Reima tore a strip off the bottom of his shirt and carefully used it to wrap up the piece of bark. Teegan laid down on the ground and Eirian and Aubree held her wing open.

"Don't touch the blood," warned Teegan, as Reima knelt beside her.

Reima nodded. "This will hurt."

Teegan closed her eyes and clenched her teeth. Reima cut. She tensed and whimpered, but did not cry out. He finished and stood. Only a remnant of skin was left on the edges of the wing-frame.

"Will you at least let me stop the bleeding?" asked Aubree. "I think I can handle that much."

Teegan nodded, eyes still closed. Aubree closed her own eyes and focused on the open vessels, willing them closed.

"Thanks," whispered Teegan.

Aubree opened her eyes. "Don't mention it." She turned to Reima. "Now, let me see your hand. Did the bark cut through?"

Reima held his hand in a fist against his chest. "A bit, but I'm fine."

"Let me see." Aubree held out her hand and waited.

Reima finally relented and let Aubree see his hand. A deep gash crossed his palm.

It did not reach muscle, but Aubree knew he would need stitches. "Reima!" exclaimed Aubree.

Without waiting for permission, Aubree stopped the bleeding and willed the skin cells to replicate until there was nothing left of the cut but a thin white line.

"That's enough." Eirian stopped Aubree from doing any more. "I understand this was necessary, but it's not a good idea to tempt fate with these powers."

"Eirian's right." Teegan groaned and folded her ruined wing against her back. "We need to get moving, anyway. Tola's minions will have seen us fall. They're probably in the forest already."

"You're still naked," Marcia pointed out.

Teegan rolled her eyes. "I really don't think there's anything I can do about that. None of us had time to pack an overnight bag."

"Here," Elior took off his shirt and handed it to Teegan. "It's not much, but it'll cover you."

Teegan took the shirt, tore the back to fit her wings, and slipped it over her head. "Thanks."

"Now can we get moving?" Eirian nervously glanced around the clearing. "I don't like this forest."

"None of us do," agreed Elior.

"Which way do we go?" asked Marcia.

Teegan turned in a slow circle.

"I – I don't know," she admitted. "I could see the way out while we flew, but I got turned around during the fight."

"It's this way." Marvin pointed through the trees.

"How do you know that?" asked Marcia. "Wait, don't tell me. The trees told you?"

Marvin nodded as Marcia turned him back around to face the group.

"How do you know we can trust the trees?" asked Aubree.

"They're not friendly trees, but I don't think we have a choice," shrugged Marvin.

"Okay. Marvin is our navigator, Reima and Teegan can help fight if needed, and Eirian is in charge," said Elior. "Aubree can be our healer, only if we have no other choice. Does this work for everyone?"

"What about you and me?" asked Marcia. "What is our job?"

"Our job is to take care of the rest of the group and make sure no one gives up hope."

"So, we're basically the group's cheerleaders?"

"Is that a problem?" asked Elior.

Marcia shook her head, took Marvin's hand, and they entered the forest.

20

Reima spent years in the Mortal Realm, trapped in a human body with human senses. He forgot the power of his natural senses, especially his nose. The Razor Wood smelled like death and rot. He knew the others smelled it too, by their crinkled noses. Marcia complained about it more than once. The odor nearly overwhelmed his sensitive nose. He tried not to show discomfort, but Aubree could tell.

"What are you going to do when we get to the palace?" she asked, trying to distract him. "You're not going to go back to the human world, are you?"

"It depends on what your father decides." Reima gently squeezed Aubree's hand. "I want to stay here, with you, but if the king says I have to leave, then I won't have a choice."

Aubree firmly nodded. "If he makes you leave, then I'm going with you."

Reima smiled and put his arm around her shoulder. "I appreciate that."

He had no intention of letting her go back to the Mortal Realm with him. She was a princess and her parents had spent enough time away from her. He said nothing.

"How much further?" pouted Marcia. "My feet are getting sore."

"I thought we were supposed to be the group's cheerleaders, not the group's complainers," joked Elior.

"I don't see you doing much cheering," teased Marcia, sticking out her tongue.

"If we are to believe the trees, then we still have a long way to go, I'm afraid," said Marvin. "We probably won't make it today."

Eirian, walking in silence, suddenly stopped. "You mean we will have to spend the night here?" she asked, panic in her voice.

Elior pulled her close. "We'll be okay. We're all together, and Tola is gone. She can't hurt you anymore."

"What about the angry group of faeries after us?" asked Marcia. "I could not understand a word any of them said, but they seemed pretty ticked off."

Teegan scoffed. "They may be angry, but they're also very stupid, most of them. They just lost their mistress. They don't know what to do without her. They'll probably give up soon, if they haven't already."

Marica suspiciously glanced at Teegan. "You sound really sure about that."

Teegan shrugged. Pain shot through her injured wing and she winced. "I used to be one of them. Thankfully, my service only lasted a couple of months. I was banished before I became totally dependent on her."

"Eirian?" Aubree walked over to her sister and put a hand on her arm. "I know you're afraid. I am too. But the longer we stand here, the longer it'll take us to get out. The longer it'll take us to get home."

Eirian looked up at Aubree, a hopeful smile on her lips. "Home. You called it home."

"Well, it is, isn't it?" asked Aubree. "Even though I was just a baby and don't remember it, it's still my home, and Mom and Dad are waiting for us."

Eirian smiled and tenderly touched Aubree's cheek. "You're right. They're waiting. Thank you."

"Would it help if I did some actual cheers?" asked Marcia as they started walking again.

"Please don't," frowned Teegan. "I'm in enough pain."

"Go ahead, Marcia," encouraged Eirian.

Teegan rolled her eyes as Marcia started going through her cheer routine. They did not worry about making too much noise. The only things that lived in the Wood were the trees, and they already knew the group was there.

Marcia's enthusiasm, though slightly forced, did seem to boost everyone's spirits. At one point, Marcia made Elior, the other cheerleader, join in. He tried to do a jump, slipped on a loose rock, and fell on his backside. Everyone burst into laughter.

"Okay, I was wrong," laughed Teegan. "I didn't think I'd like the cheers, but that did make me feel better."

"Are you okay, Love?" chuckled Eirian, holding out a hand to help him up.

Elior allowed Eirian to pull him to his feet. "I'm fine. Just a bruised ego. I think I'm done with the cheers for now, Marcia."

"You just need more practice." Marcia easily performed the move that Elior failed.

"I think that's enough with the cheers," said Teegan. "Why don't we sing or something instead."

"Yeah, you can sing us some of the songs you used to sing at your speakeasy," suggested Reima.

"You had a speakeasy?" asked Marcia, walking backwards to face Teegan. "I bet you have all sorts of stories from then."

Teegan shook her head. "That was a long time ago."

"Come on, Teegan." Eirian nudged her friend on her uninjured shoulder. "I've heard you sing. You're amazing."

Teegan relented. "Fine. I'll sing one song, and, maybe, if you're lucky, I'll tell you some stories from that time."

Their spirits faded by midday. The care they took to avoid the razor-sharp bark of the trees dissipated the further they traveled. They grew tired, hungry, and thirsty. They found no food or water along their journey.

"What kind of forest doesn't at least have a stream?" asked Marcia.

"There must be water somewhere," said Eirian. "Otherwise the trees would be dead."

"The trees know where the water is, but they won't tell me. They want us to die here." Marvin shuddered. "They say that death nourishes them."

"Of course, it does," muttered Teegan.

"Wait, if the trees want us to die, then how do we know they're sending us in the right direction?" asked Marcia. "How do we know they aren't leading us around in circles?"

"We don't," said Marvin.

"What if I scout ahead?" asked Reima. "I can get into wolf form. My nose is stronger in that form. And see if I can smell anything."

"But, if your nose is stronger when you're in wolf form, then won't it magnify the stench of the forest?" asked Aubree.

"Yes," admitted Reima. "But a wolf's nose is made to sift through smells. I can't do that right now."

Eirian nodded. "I think he should do it. We can go a little while without food or water, but it will take us longer to get out if we're dehydrated. Besides, we don't know how much farther we have to go, or what we will find when we finally do get out."

"I'm going to have to take off my clothes. I don't want them to get destroyed like Teegan's did," said Reima. "I'll need someone to carry them for me."

"I'll carry them," offered Aubree.

The girls turned their heads while Reima stripped. He folded his clothes and set them in a pile for Aubree to carry. He got down onto his hands and knees and changed. His bones crunched as they changed size and shape. Fur sprouted all over his body. His face stretched into a muzzle. The entire change took only a few seconds. When he finished, he shook himself.

"He's done," said Elior, to the girls.

"Oh my gosh!" exclaimed Marcia. "He's so cute!"

"Back off, he's all mine," laughed Aubree. She came over and put a hand on his head. "Can you talk like this?" she asked.

Reima shook his head.

"Dragons are the only ones who can speak with their thoughts," explained Teegan. "But he can still understand us."

"This is strange," said Aubree. "It's going to take me a while to get used to the fact that this is all real. My friend is a dragon that I can ride, and my boyfriend is a dog."

Reima growled in annoyance.

"Wolf, sorry." Aubree corrected herself. "Part of me feels as if this is all a dream."

She started to scratch Reima behind the ears. He closed his eyes and wagged his tail.

Aubree laughed. "You sure act like a dog."

Reima shook his head from side to side. *Focus.* He told himself. He nudged his clothes with his nose. Aubree got the hint and picked them up.

"Do you smell anything?" asked Elior.

Reima put his nose to the ground and sniffed around. The stench of rot grew worse, but he ignored it. He smelled his friends and his own scent on his clothes. He tried harder and picked out a slightly familiar scent. He concentrated on that scent, holding it in his nose. The smell hit him; fish! Fish meant not only food, but water too.

He lifted his head and made a sound in his throat to get the attention of the others.

"Did you find something?" Aubree hopefully asked.

Reima nodded and started through the trees, following the scent. The others followed.

"What do you smell?" asked Marcia.

"He can't answer," said Teegan.

"Oh, right."

The smell of fish got stronger, and eventually, he heard the sound of running water.

"Do you hear that?" asked Eirian.

"It's water," said Aubree.

Their pace quickened. They hurried after Reima until they came to a stream. Unlike the rest of the forest, the water rushing through the stream looked clear and clean.

"Do you think it's safe to drink?" asked Marcia.

Reima leaned down and sniffed the water. He did not smell anything foul. He leaned down and carefully dipped in his tongue. Everyone waited for his reaction. He raised his head and nodded to the others before drinking more heartily.

"It's good," Aubree sighed in relief.

She knelt down beside Reima and scooped up some water with her hands. The others followed suit.

"It must run down from those mountains." Eirian nodded upstream.

"I guess even Tola and her army need fresh water," said Elior.

Reima moved downstream to catch some fish. He gathered enough for everyone and brought them to the group.

"Thanks, Reima." Aubree scratched him behind the ears.

He rubbed his head against her arm and then pawed the ground near his clothes. Aubree nodded and carried the pile away from the group so Reima could change back in private.

"Do we have to eat these fish raw, or what?" asked Marcia.

"You have a problem with sushi?" asked Reima, rejoining the group in his bi-pedal form.

Teegan laughed. "No one has to eat sushi. I can cook the fish. I may not be able to fly, but I can still breathe fire."

"Is there enough room for you to change right here?" asked Aubree.

"Who said anything about changing?"

Teegan told them to put the fish into a pile. She exhaled a jet of flame and cooked the fish with a single breath. Marcia yelped in surprise and jumped away from Teegan.

They rested and ate their fill. Marvin presented their next problem. "The trees are angry with us for finding the stream, and they're refusing to tell me the way out."

"What are we going to do now?" asked Marcia.

Eirian looked at the stream, and then looked through the trees. "This stream is fresh water. It didn't originate from here. If we follow the stream, it should lead us out."

"Plus, we won't have to worry about food or water," added Elior.

"What if it steers us off course?" asked Marcia.

"It's not like we were following much of a course in the first place," Teegan pointed out.

21

The rest of their trip through the wood was uneventful. The stream provided food, water, and a point of reference. The babbling brook lulled them to sleep when they stopped for the night. They continued the next morning, exhausted. Their spirits lifted when they emerged from the shadow of the trees into bright sunlight.

"We made it out," sighed Eirian. She closed her eyes and let the sun warm her face.

"Those are the Mountains of May'Edor," pointed Teegan. "That's where I was hatched. We should avoid going that way. My parents may still live up there, and we do not want to run into them."

"The palace is over that way, anyway." Eirian pointed in a different direction.

"You recognize where we are?" asked Aubree.

Eirian shook her head. "Not personally, but part of my schooling involved looking at maps of the kingdom. If those are the Mountains of May'Edor, then this is the Lairith Valley, and the palace is down that way. I don't remember the Razor Wood being on any of those maps, though."

"If I remember correctly, it was the Bruviel Forest that bordered the Lairith Valley," said Elior.

"It is the Bruviel. Look." Teegan jerked her head in the direction they just left.

They turned to face the wood. A large, pristine, pine forest replaced the black trees of the Razor Wood.

"What just happened?" asked Marcia. "Where'd the creepy forest go?"

"Elior, do you remember when we were doing all that research on Tola, before Aubree was born?" asked Eirian.

"Yeah, what about it?"

"None of the books we read could agree on one location for the Razor Wood. Tola and the Wood just appeared whenever someone wanted to make a deal."

"When I was working for her, she told me to fly in the opposite direction of the sun until I saw her palace," said Teegan. "It didn't matter if the sun was in the East or the West. Sometimes I flew for hours, sometimes only a few minutes."

Marica tilted her head to one side. "But Mom said that your father's guards were watching her. How could they have been watching her if the Wood doesn't stay in the same place?"

"Because she knew they were looking for her," said Aubree. "She knew they would be keeping an eye on her, and that Dad would try to change the deal, so she let them find her."

No one said anything for a while after that, each thinking how lucky they really were that they defeated Tola.

"Hey!" called a voice. "Are you folks okay?"

A bay centaur leading a large cart stopped in the middle of the road. Eirian walked over to the centaur and motioned for the others to follow.

"You all look like you have been through a lot," said the centaur.

Eirian glanced at the group and hastily agreed. Everyone had tangled hair and dirty clothes. Elior shivered without a shirt and Teegan wore *only* a shirt – Elior's shirt.

Eirian mirthlessly chuckled. "You have no idea."

"My name is Telnaam," said the centaur. "Is there anything I can do for you? I have warm, clean clothes and water if you want to clean up. Where are you headed?"

"You are very kind." Eirian bowed her head in thanks.

Telnaam unhitched himself from his cart and went around to the side. He unfolded the side into a merchant's stall. He walked around to the back and dug through chests of cloth. He looked up every now and again, as if judging sizes, and eventually returned with a stack of clothes. He handed a small pile to each person.

"There's a bucket of water back there, with a cloth for you to wash with," said Telnaam. "It's not particularly glamorous, but you can at least rid yourselves of some of that dirt, and I've untied the curtains so you can have privacy."

"Thank you," said Eirian, after translating his offer into English for Marcia and Marvin. "We don't have any money right now, but once we reach the capital, I can send some to you."

"That's quite alright, Miss," said Telnaam. "I'm just happy to help. I hope the clothes fit." Teegan walked to the back of the stall. Telnaam nodded her way. "You may have to cut the back of it to accommodate your wings." He turned back to Eirian. "You are going to the capital, you say? I'm heading that way myself. I would be glad of the company, if you are willing to travel with a stranger."

Eirian smiled in thanks. "Of course. Allow me to introduce my party, and forgive me for not doing so sooner. The dragon in your cart is called Teegan, and this is Reima, Marvin, Marcia, Elior, and Aubree." Eirian gestured to each as she named them. "And I am Eirian."

"Eirian?" repeated Telnaam. "You have the same name as the Princess. Wait a moment." Telnaam leaned in for a closer look and Eirian stood up straighter. The centaur's eyes widened with recognition, and he bowed with the human half of his body. "Y-your Highness, p-please forgive me for not recognizing you sooner," Telnaam stammered.

Eirian shook her head. "It's alright. After all that's happened, I don't think I would recognize myself."

"If you don't mind my asking, Your Highness," Telnaam straightened, "where have you been? No one has seen or heard from you in years and the king and queen refuse to talk about it. There are rumors that you died."

"I had to leave," said Eirian. "I'm sure my parents will make an official announcement when they learn that we are safe, but, as you have been kind enough to help us, I will tell you. For the last sixteen years, I have been in the Mortal Realm."

"For what reason, if I may ask?"

Eirian paused. "That is a long story. Before I begin, I would ask that you keep to yourself what I am about to tell you until after the official announcement has been made. I am not afraid our enemies will hear, they already know that we are back, but I would like to reach the palace in peace."

"I understand, Your Highness." Telnaam bowed again.

"Please, just call me Eirian. I don't want my presence known quite yet."

Telnaam agreed to this, and after every one had cleaned up, and changed into clean clothes, they all continued down the road to the capital. Telnaam listened closely while Eirian told her story. When she finished, he told the group, with Eirian translating from Common to English, what happened in the kingdom while they were gone.

"We first noticed something was wrong when the king and queen closed the gates of the palace to the public," said Telnaam. "Shortly after that, the number of guards patrolling the streets and, in the cities, increased. They knocked on doors and asked questions. I don't know what they asked other people, but I was stopped by a handful of guards when I was on the road. They asked me my name, where I had come from, and where I was going. Then they asked me where I got my wares. After I answered all their questions, they handed me a slip of paper to show any other guards if they tried to stop me."

Telnaam reached into a bag he wore across his chest and handed a piece of paper to Eirian. It stated that the carrier had been cleared of all suspicion. It was signed by Devin and bore the royal seal.

"Did they tell you what the suspicion was?" asked Eirian, handing Telnaam back his paper.

Telnaam shook his head. "They wouldn't tell us anything. I was stopped more times than I can count during those first few weeks, but they never gave me any trouble. I handed them the paper, and they let me on my way. There were more people on the roads as well, all carrying bags like they were leaving for good, but they were always alone. I recognized some of them. Some of them had families that they left behind. There were whispers that those people worked for Tola and they were leaving the cities and villages before the guards caught them. From the story you just told me, I guess that was true."

"Which way were they going?" asked Elior.

"All different ways," answered Telnaam. "Some went North, some East, some took off flying, some melted into streams and rivers."

"Yet they were all going to the same place," said Teegan.

"I didn't even know Tola was real," said Telnaam. "I thought she was just a story. Something made up to keep children from running off on their own."

"Well, we don't have to worry about her anymore." Aubree surprised everyone by speaking Common. "She's gone now, and she's not coming back."

22

By the end of the week, they had reached the borders of the White Forest. The sight of the familiar trees filled Eirian with hope. Eirian gazed Westward at the familiar bright orange and purple sunset. She inhaled the sweet scent of Dusk Daisies. Telnaam led the group to a common traveler's campsite just inside the darkening forest. He passed out the bedrolls they used for the last few nights. Reima and Elior gathered sticks and branches to make a fire. Teegan lit it with a snort.

"Just think, tomorrow night, I will be able to eat dinner in the dining hall of the palace and sleep in my own bed," said Eirian as they finished dinner. "Only one more day before I get to see Mama and Daddy again. Oh! I cannot wait to be home."

"You have a lot to tell them when we get there." Elior put one hand on Eirian's belly and kissed her on the cheek.

Eirian leaned into him. "I know. I'm counting on Daddy being too happy that we are back to be angry at us for getting married like we did."

"Sounds like a plan," laughed Elior.

"Aubree, are you okay?" asked Reima.

Aubree, her food barely touched, silently stared into the flames.

"I'm just nervous," she admitted. "I've been thinking about how much my life has changed. A few months ago, I thought I was just a normal girl who lost her parents as a baby. I didn't really have any big plans. I wanted to graduate from school and start a family. I didn't even know what kind of job I wanted. Now, all of a sudden, I'm anything but normal. Not only am I not an orphan, I'm not even human. I am an elf princess who was forced into hiding because some psycho wanted me for these powers, I never knew I had. On top of that, my cousin isn't my cousin. She, my boyfriend, and his best friend, are all faeries."

Eirian put her arm around her sister.

Aubree leaned into the touch. "I'm sorry, Ana. I know none of this is your fault. It's just different. And I guess I can't call you Ana anymore, can I? That's going to be hard."

"You can still call me Ana," Eirian assured her. "I know this is hard. Change is hard. I remember how hard it was for me when I first got to the Mortal Realm, but you'll get used to it, and you won't be alone."

"What if our father doesn't let Reima stay?"

Eirian took a deep breath.

"I can't guarantee that he will," admitted Eirian, "but I will do everything in my power to convince him."

"I just don't know how I'm going to find someone to replace him at the café." Teegan playfully punched Reima on the shoulder.

"Ow!" Reima rubbed his shoulder. "Be careful. You've got your strength back, remember?"

"Baby." Teegan stuck out her tongue.

"I think we're all going to be okay," said Marcia. "No matter where we all are, we'll be okay."

Aubree smiled and hugged her. Eirian hugged them both. Elior and Reima joined in and Teegan grabbed Marvin and Telnaam by the shoulders and pulled them into the group hug. With Teegan's wings poking people in the face, and Telnaam's horse end sticking out, it was a very awkward hug, but no one complained.

"Now I think it's time for sleep," said Telnaam. "We'll have to wake early if we want to reach the capital before noon tomorrow."

Aubree was too nervous to sleep. She tossed and turned on her bedroll for a while before giving up. The fire burned low, but was still warm, thanks to it being lit with dragon flame. She looked across to the other side of the camp, where Reima slept. She shivered in the cool Autumn breeze. She wondered about her future.

What does it mean to be a Princess? How many rules will I have to learn? I don't know anything about this place, about faeries.

She stared at Reima, peaceful in the glow of embers.

What about him? What if the king – my father – makes Reima go back? Can I go back with him? Will I be allowed to go back? I don't want to live here without him. I won't *live here without him.* She sighed, pulling the blanket tighter around her neck. *Am I selfish for even thinking this – after what everyone went through to protect me?* Aubree rolled over to face her sister.

Eirian slept close to Elior, his arms wrapped around her. One hand rested on Eirian's belly. *Eirian seemed convinced Father will let Reima stay, but will he? If he's anything like Eirian and Elior, there should be no problem, but –*

Aubree shook her head. "Ari– Eirian knows them," she said to herself. "She grew up with them. If she says that it'll be okay, then it'll be okay."

Aubree looked over at Marcia, sleeping beside her. *Marcia doesn't have anything to worry about. She isn't royal, and her boyfriend isn't an exile.*

"Ana said that she would talk to our parents," whispered Aubree. "I trust her."

Aubree closed her eyes. This time, sleep easily came.

The next day's walk through the White Forest was much different than their trek through the Razor Wood. This wood, though not nearly as quiet as Tola's home, was much more peaceful. Birds sang and animals darted through the trees ahead of them. Dryads and other tree spirits whispered to each other as the group passed. Aubree caught the words "princess" and "alive", along with Eirian's name, in various languages. She shook her head, not exactly certain how she understood them.

A curious pair of tiny, winged sprites flew up to them and fluttered around Eirian's head. One of them picked up a handful of her hair and the other one flew around to examine the others in the group. After a few minutes, the second sprite joined the first one. They chattered excitedly to each other in their high, squeaky voices. They took hands and flew off into the trees.

Telnaam chuckled. "So much for keeping your arrival secret. The whole forest will know by nightfall."

"We'll be home before then," replied Eirian, untangling the knot the sprite tied in her hair. "They'll most likely tell the outer cities and villages first, since the capital will be the first to know."

Eirian caught the eye of a dryad. The creature nodded and melted into her tree.

"The last time I was in this forest, Mama and I were on our way to the Winter Palace, right after I told her about Tola," said Eirian.

"You don't think they could be there, do you?" asked Elior. "At the Winter Palace? That is where we left from and Winter isn't far off."

"According to the trees, no one has been to the Winter Palace since you left," said Marvin. "These trees are much friendlier than the other ones, by the way.

Marica smiled at Marvin and wrapped one arm around him. She turned to Eirian. "If you left from there, doesn't that mean that the gate is there?"

"Faerie regents can open gates anywhere," explained Eirian. "Tears and other holes are stationary, as are the main gates, but not the one we came through."

"Then how did Mom and Aunt Charity get through?"

"Through the main gate, most likely," said Eirian.

"But Tola sealed those," said Marcia. "Why couldn't you or Aubree just open new gates? You're royalty."

"Yes," agreed Eirian, "but we didn't have powers in the Mortal Realm. If we had entered through the main gates, then I could have made us come out wherever I wanted."

"Aubree had powers." Marcia jerked her head toward Aubree. "Aubree still has powers."

"Powers that I don't know how to use and that I don't want," countered Aubree.

"I definitely need to talk to Daddy about that," said Eirian. "He'll know what to do."

"You won't have to wait much longer." Elior pointed ahead. "Look."

The trees thinned ahead of them. Aubree saw the gates of the capital city. Butterflies filled her stomach at the sight of them. Her trembling hand found Reima's steady one and she gripped it for comfort.

Reima gave Aubree's hand a gentle squeeze.

The large wooden gates stood wide open with a guard on either side.

One guard held out his hand. "Papers."

Telnaam handed the guard his paper. The guard looked it over, nodded, and handed it back.

"What about your companions?" he asked.

Eirian took a deep breath before straightening and walking up to the guard.

"Princess!" exclaimed the guard. He stood straighter.

The other guard hurried over. "Princess Eirian! Is it really you?"

Eirian dipped her head in a deep nod. "Yes. I am back."

"Garrick, go get the Captain," ordered the first guard.

"Wait, how do we know it truly is the princess and not some trick from the enchantress?" asked Garrick.

"I am afraid I have no proof," said Eirian, "other than my word and the word of my companions. I would present my ring, bearing the royal seal, but I am afraid I did not bring it with me when I went into hiding."

"That, I believe is proof itself," came a new voice. "For the enchantress would not have known that and would have attempted to recreate the ring. She cannot, however, recreate your beauty, Your Highness."

"Devin!" Eirian, forgetting her regal composure, ran to embrace the newcomer.

Devin laughed and returned Eirian's embrace. Marcia's ears perked at the sound of the man's name, the only word she understood, and she gripped Marvin's hand.

"It fills me with immense pleasure to see you again, Your Highness." Devin returned Eirian's hug. "Your parents will be relieved as well, to find you safe." He turned to the two guards. "Garrick, send word to the palace; the princess has returned."

"Yes, sir!" Garrick saluted Devin and turned to Eirian. "My apologies for not believing you, Your Highness."

"You are forgiven," said Eirian. "You were just doing your job."

Garrick bowed his head, then turned to complete his orders. Devin turned to the others. He faced Marcia, and his eyes filled with tears.

"Hello, Marcia," he said in broken English. "Do you remember me? I'm sorry my English is rusty."

"You're my father," she whispered.

Devin smiled. "Yes, I am."

Marcia leaned forward and threw her arms around him.

He returned the embrace. "I have missed you so much. Not a day passed when I did not think of you and wonder what kind of woman you had become."

They stayed like that for several minutes before reluctantly pulling away. Marcia introduced Marvin to Devin.

"Yes, I have heard about you from Claudette." Devin shook Marvin's hand. "Thank you for taking care of Marcia."

"You've heard from Mom?" asked Marcia. "Where is she? Is she okay?"

Devin nodded. "She's fine. She and Charity are at the palace. She will be extremely pleased to see you well." Devin turned to Elior. "Elior, it seems like the king put his faith in the right man. Well done." Devin saluted Elior.

"Thank you, Sir." Elior saluted in return.

"I take it this young lady is Princess Aubree." Devin turned and bowed. "I am pleased to see you safe as well, Your Highness."

"Thank you," said Aubree, slightly embarrassed at the formal introduction.

Eirian introduced the rest of the group to Devin, leaving out the parts about Reima and Teegan being exiles, although the look on his face hinted that he already knew Teegan.

"I am anxious to hear your story, Your Highness," began Devin, once again speaking Common. "I have heard only parts of it from Claudette, but I know you must be even more anxious to get home. I will hold my tongue and wait until then. Now, if you would permit me, I will escort you through the city and to the palace."

"If you will excuse me, Your Highness." Telnaam spoke up. "I am afraid this is where we must part. I was happy to be your escort through the forest, but I need to find a place to set up my stall."

Eirian nodded. She took Telnaam's hand. "Of course. It was a pleasure to meet you, Telnaam, and I thank you for escorting us. When I get settled, I will see to it that you are reimbursed for the clothes and rewarded for your generosity."

"I would not dare refuse the kindness of the Princess." Telnaam bowed, and, after bidding the others goodbye, walked down the main street.

Devin turned to Aubree and gestured in the direction of the palace.

"Now, Princess, are you ready to meet your parents?"

Hidden Identity

23

Word traveled quickly. The scene at the city gate attracted the eyes and ears of everyone nearby. Devin cleared the way for Aubree and the rest to travel through the crowded streets. He kept Marcia close by his side. The citizens and merchants whispered to each other, staring at the group like the creatures in the forest.

Aubree saw the palace; a dazzling, white structure glittering in the sunlight. The closer they got; the bigger the pit in Aubree's stomach grew. She squeezed Reima's hand for comfort.

"Everything will be okay," he whispered to her.

She wished she felt as certain. The great gates of the palace loomed before them – tall silver gates, decorated with silver vines sprouting silver flowers. Hundreds of silver butterflies perched on the sculpted flowers. Aubree gasped. Her gaze went from the magnificent gates to the palace courtyard, made of white stone, just as Eirian described. A fountain sat in the middle of the courtyard and a stone maiden stood in the center, pouring water over a stone garden.

"Eirian!" called a voice from across the courtyard.

A woman in a flowing white dress, carrying her long, silver hair over one arm to prevent herself from tripping over it with her bare feet, ran to them.

"Mama!" Eirian broke away from the group and ran to meet her mother.

Close behind the queen ran the king. He wrapped his arms around both women.

"Mommy!" yelled Marcia, as she spotted Claudette and Charity.

She kept hold of Marvin and her father's hands as she ran to embrace her mother and aunt.

Elior ran to meet another Elf woman; his mother.

Aubree kept her grip on Reima's hand and watched Eirian interact with her parents. She would have known who they were even without Eirian calling to them. It was more than a visual resemblance. There was a familiarity to them.

A memory flashed through her mind. A kind, lovely face, eyes wet with tears, leaning closer to kiss her forehead. A soft voice in a familiar language whispering: "Do not be afraid, little one. I am putting you in the best hands."

A new face, just as kind, just as sad. A different voice, this one deeper: "Your sister is brave and strong. She will keep you safe."

Tears streamed down Aubree's face as she opened her eyes and looked to where Eirian spoke with her parents. They glanced up. Aubree's eyes met those of Queen Livia. Her fear melted. She released Reima's hand and ran straight into the waiting arms of her mother and father.

"Mommy," she sobbed. "Daddy."

She did not say anything more as the arms wrapped around her. A hole in her heart, that she did not know she had, filled. She laughed and cried at the same time. *This is where I belong.*

She knew that, eventually, she would have to let go. They would break the embrace to let Eirian tell them about everything that had happened, but not yet. Not just yet. Right now, she was home.

Aubree sat with her parents on a large sofa in a sitting room that was bigger than the living room and kitchen combined back at the house. Marvin, Marcia, Devin, Claudette, and Charity sat on another sofa, Reima and Teegan each sat in an armchair, and Elior sat between his mother and Eirian on a smaller sofa while they told Livia and Alberic the events of the past sixteen years.

The king and queen sat, quietly listening, exchanging looks with each other at times, but never interrupting. Eirian left nothing out. She hesitated at times, like when she told of her feelings and current relationship status with Elior. She feared her parents' reactions. Alberic and Livia only nodded and encouraged her to continue.

Eirian came to the encounter with Tola in the café. She told her side, and then paused for Aubree to tell hers. Eirian continued, taking back over to tell about what happened after.

Eirian finished her story, and waited. The king and queen contemplated the story in silence for several minutes, processing everything they just heard.

Finally, Alberic spoke. "I see that much has happened these past years," he began, "and I would like to address several points in your story." Aubree shot a nervous glance at Reima. "First of all, Eirian, it is clear that Livia and I brought you up to be a wise woman who makes wise decisions. Therefore, I will ease your mind by saying that I will not go back on any of the decisions that you have made, though I would like to speak with Elior and Reima privately when we are finished here."

Both couples sighed in relief.

"As you wish, Your Majesty." Elior's voice did little to conceal the joy that showed on his face.

"Thank you for your kindness," added Reima, bowing his head.

"As for you, dragon." Alberic turned to Teegan. "I appreciate your willingness to return to exile, but I believe, based on your actions towards my daughters and your assistance in their mission, that you have rightly served your time and more than made up for your crimes. You are free to remain here, if you so choose."

Teegan looked up in disbelief, speechless. She fell out of her chair and knelt before the king. "Your Majesty, this kindness is more than I deserve. I am eternally grateful and will try, for the rest of my days, to show you that this gift of mercy will not be wasted."

Alberic held up a hand. "That is not necessary. All I ask is that you continue to be someone that my daughters can rely upon."

"I promise, My Lord." Teegan returned to her seat.

Alberic turned to Livia.

"Do you have anything to add, my love, before I move on?" he asked.

Livia nodded and turned to Marcia. "Marcia, I would like to commend you. I know this was not easy for you.

None of this had anything to with you, but you were caught up in the middle, just the same. You were brought up to believe that you were something you were not, as was Aubree. I cannot imagine how you must have felt when you discovered the truth, but you handled it well, and you gave Aubree someone to talk to and confide in, and for that I thank you."

Marcia blushed and bowed her head.

Alberic clapped his hands. "Now, on to more serious matters. Tola is gone, but her magic remains. We must find a way to rid Aubree of these dangerous powers, as well as find a way to unseal the gates."

"That has already been taken care of."

Aubree turned to the door of the sitting room to see a faerie woman standing in the doorway. She had bright red hair and wore an orange gown that resembled something out of the fifteenth century. Her white wings sparkled as if studded with diamonds.

"Your Majesty, the High Queen," said Livia in a tone of reverence.

She and the others who recognized the newcomer immediately left their seats to bow before her. Aubree and Marcia looked at each other before they, as well as Marvin, followed suit.

The High Queen bid them to rise.

"Your Majesty, to what do we owe the honor of your presence?" asked Alberic.

"Who's the High Queen?" Marcia whispered to her mother, who shushed her.

The High Queen gave Marcia a warm smile. "It is alright. There are many kingdoms in this world, each with its own rulers. The position of High King or High

Queen governs them all. I am the High Queen that keeps the other kings and queens under control."

"So, you're like, in charge of this whole world?" Marcia asked.

"Yes. I am."

"Your Majesty, I have been looking to seek an audience with you for some time," said Alberic.

"I know you have, and I have not been ignoring you. Sit down, please, I have a story to tell you." The High Queen moved to sit down in one of the arm chairs, but a whimper from outside the room caused her to pause. "Oh! I almost forgot! I have something that belongs to you." She stepped into the hall and returned a moment later followed by a fat, fluffy creature.

"Winston!" exclaimed Aubree. She scooped up the puppy and laughed as he covered her face in wet kisses. She looked up to the High Queen. "Thank you."

"I had someone keep an eye on him while you were making your way here," said the High Queen. "Your neighbor, in fact. When I heard that you had arrived, I sent for your pet." She motioned again for everyone to sit and Livia told a servant to bring refreshments.

"I have been High Queen for a long time," the faerie began, "longer than I can remember. However, I have not always been so. There was a time I was simply Reya. I worked with my father on his farm until the High King saw me and took me as his wife. I loved him dearly and was very happy with him. Some time ago, he passed on, for even immortal fae do not always live forever." She paused; her eyes distant as if lost in memory. "A short time after that, my grief became so great, I began looking for someone to replace me as High Queen so that I could join him. As I had no children, my heir had to come from somewhere else. I scoured the lands for one hundred years before I found, what I believed at the time, to be the one. She was the youngest daughter of a Duke, and had the bearing of royalty. I offered her the opportunity to learn from me, and she accepted. I took her to my palace and set her up as my heir.

"The position of High Queen is one of great power, and she needed something to draw that power from. The girl had a comb made of crystal, her most prized possession, and I poured into that comb all the powers she would need to someday rule, just as my husband had done for me, the day he made he his queen."

"You're talking about Tola, aren't you?" asked Aubree.

The High Queen nodded. "It was not long before I discovered that she had been studying dark and forbidden magic," she continued. "I tried to warn her of the dangers of studying such things, but she ignored me. I finally had to issue her an ultimatum: Stop studying dark magic, or relinquish her new position as my heir."

"I bet that went over like a lead balloon," muttered Marcia. Claudette again shushed her.

"She refused both options, saying that if I would not continue to train her, then she would leave and train on her own until she was strong enough to overthrow me by force. I tried to stop her by appealing to her former nature, the innocent girl she was when we first met, but that girl was no more. She had been consumed by greed and lust for power. When she left, I tried to search for her, but she shielded herself from me. I began to hear her name in connection with the Razor Wood, a place that had been missing since before my husband was born. I knew then, that I would never be able to find her on my own, for the Razor Wood is a dark place, beyond the reach of all things good and pure."

"What does all this have to do with me?" asked Aubree.

The High Queen turned to her. "You know why Tola wanted you, yes? You saw it in her eyes when she looked at you."

Aubree nodded.

"That is only part of the reason. Tola's powers, great as they were, were limited. She was not strong enough to overthrow me on her own. She wanted to train you, to teach you as I taught her, and then use you to gain control of the entire world."

"But why?"

"Because, you are the one I have been waiting for. I was foolish and impatient when I began my search for an heir. I looked only for someone who appeared, on the surface, to be wise and strong enough to take my place. I did not pause to look inside for the one thing that is required. My husband saw it in me when he married me, and I see it, now, in you. Tola saw it too, before you were ever born, and plotted to take you for herself. That is why you were able to defeat her. Her powers came from me, and sprang from a selfish desire. Your powers come from inside you."

The entire room fell silent following the High Queen's words. Winston squirmed in Aubree's arms and whimpered for her to put him down.

"What are you saying?" asked Alberic in a quiet voice. "Are you saying that Aubree is to be the next High

Queen? That I am to lose my daughter again the very day she returns home to me?"

"Fear not, young king." The High Queen offered Alberic a kind smile. "Aubree is the one to take over as High Queen, someday, but that day is still far off. Should she choose to accept, she will need many years of lessons on how to control her powers, instead of fearing them, and to use them for the good of this world. She will be allowed to live here, with you, but she must come to my palace daily for her lessons, just as she would if she were going to school in the Mortal Realm."

"Should I choose to accept?" repeated Aubree, her voice barely above a whisper. "I have a choice?"

The High Queen smiled. "Of course, you do, my dear. I am not going to force you into anything."

"Do I have to answer right now?"

"No. You need time to adjust to living in this world before you have to worry about ruling it," replied the High Queen.

Eirian spoke up. "I have a question, Your Majesty. When Tola found us in the café, she said that she would be willing to let Aubree stay, if I gave her my unborn child. Does that mean that my baby will have the same powers?"

The High Queen shook her head. "I am afraid not. When Tola made that offer, she was giving you a false choice. She knew you would never give up your child."

"She was bluffing?" asked Marcia.

"Yes. She was bluffing," said the High Queen. "That does not mean that your child will not be special, Princess."

Eirian smiled and put a hand to her stomach. "Thank you."

"One thing still bothers me," said Marcia. "You all said that this 'Veil' makes it that no one can use their powers in the human world."

The High Queen nodded. "That is correct."

"Then how did Tola keep her powers?" asked Marcia.

"That is a good question," said the High Queen. "I am afraid that I am the one to blame for Tola's ability to retain her magic. The magic of the High Ruler overrides that of the Veil, for it was a High King that created the Veil to separate the two worlds."

"She could keep her powers because she had the magic of a High Queen?" asked Aubree.

"Yes," said the High Queen. "That is why you were able to bring Teegan back, as well. You have always had your powers, Aubree. You simply did not know how to access them. For example, when you arrived, you could already understand the tongues of others, could you not?" The High Queen switched to Elvish. "You can understand me right now, can you not?"

"You can teach me how to safely use my powers?" asked Aubree in Elvish, answering the High Queen's questions as a result.

"Yes, if you wish to learn." The High Queen switched back to English.

"What about Reima?" asked Aubree. "What will happen to him if I agree to become High Queen?"

The High Queen smiled. "I think you already know the answer to that question."

She rose from her chair, the rest of the room following suit.

"Before I take my leave, I do have one more matter to address." The High Queen turned to Teegan. "Since you are no longer banished, I expect you will soon long to fly again and regret ruining your wing. Would you like me to repair it for you?"

Teegan glanced over her shoulder before turning back to the High Queen.

"What would you want in exchange?" she warily asked.

"Nothing, dear, nothing," the High Queen assured her. "I am not like Tola. I do not require deals or payment. I am offering as a gift, completely free, no strings attached."

Teegan looked hesitant, but stretched out her wing, nonetheless. Marcia and Marvin moved out of the way. The High Queen touched Teegan's wing with one hand. The appendage brightly glowed. The High Queen removed her hand, revealing a completely healed wing.

"You made it look so easy." Aubree remembered how hard she had to concentrate to make anything happen.

The High Queen smiled. "I have had lots of practice. Someday, if you choose to come learn from me, you will be able to heal entire armies without thinking about it. Thank you, Your Majesties, for opening your home to me." She nodded to Alberic and Livia, before she left the room.

"Well, this has been an exciting day," said Queen Livia. "My daughters have returned to me, though very different than when they left, the High Queen in my sitting room, and my youngest chosen as her heir."

"There is still much to do before the day is over," said King Alberic. "A feast must be prepared in celebration of our reunited family, and an official announcement made, but before any of that, I wish to speak to Reima and Elior, separately. Please, follow me to my office."

Reima gave Aubree an encouraging smile before following Alberic and Elior into the hall.

"While he is doing that, I will have someone prepare chambers for our unexpected guests. Eirian, my love, I am sure you are eager to revisit your home. Would you like to include those who have never been here, or were too young to remember, in your tour?"

"Only if you come, too, Mama," said Eirian. "I have spent too much time away from you to part now."

Livia smiled as if that was exactly what she wanted to hear.

"Of course."

24

Eirian retired to her bedroom after leading a tour of the palace. The tour awakened many memories; she broke into tears more than once. Everything appeared the same as she left it that day before her escape to the Winter Palace. She sat on her bed and saw her reflection in the mirror. The face that stared back at her was familiar, but different. Her silver hair hung loose over her shoulders and the points of her ears showed through, but there was little left of the child she remembered. Her features were sharper and her eyes reflected all she had been through. She raised a hand to her face, and saw on her finger, the ring she had worn since the day she married Elior. A smile spread across her face and she dropped her hand to her abdomen, which would soon begin to grow. Yes, she went through a lot, but good still came from it.

There was a soft knock and Elior entered. "I thought I might find you in here." He sat down beside her on the bed.

"What did my father say to you?" Eirian leaned her head on his shoulder.

"Just dad stuff."

Eirian sat up and looked at Elior. "What is that supposed to mean?"

Elior shrugged. "Basically, he fussed at me for not saying anything about how I felt about you earlier and for going behind his back. Not just in marrying you, but also in everything else while we were still here."

Eirian made a face.

"But then he started telling me the standard 'take care of her,' 'treat her well,' dad stuff. He knows I will, and do, but he just had to say it out of fatherly duty. Then he actually hugged me and welcomed me to the family."

Eirian laughed. "Yeah, that whole, serious king thing is pretty much just for our subjects. When you get down to it, he's just a man. A good man and a good father."

"And an excited future grandfather," added Elior. "He said that if we have a boy, we have to name it after him, but I told him we were having a girl and naming her after my mother."

"How did he respond to that?"

"He made me promise anyway," said Elior. "For the next one."

"That sounds like a plan." Eirian leaned forward and gave Elior a passionate kiss. "We're home."

Elior held Eirian close. "We're home."

Aubree did not have a chance to think about the High Queen's offer for several weeks. That first day of their return ended with the entire kingdom celebrating. Alberic declared it to be a national holiday. Reima and Teegan were given official pardons and moved into the palace. Then came the planning for a royal celebration of Eirian and Elior's marriage and the announcement of Eirian's pregnancy.

Devin and his men were sent out to round up Tola's followers, a task harder than it seemed. After Aubree and the others left the Razor Wood, the dark forest and all who lived there vanished into thin air. No one controlled the Razer Wood with Tola gone. The High Queen said that Tola's followers were still around and would be able to leave the wood whenever they chose, but hoped they were smart enough not to.

Aubree adjusted to her new life more quickly than she thought she would.

"It was in your blood the whole time," said Eirian.

The hardest part was when Marcia told her that she was going back to the Mortal Realm with Marvin and Charity.

"Are you sure you want to go?" asked Aubree on the day they left.

Marcia nodded. "I can't get used to living here. Yes, it is beautiful, and yes, I will miss you and Eirian and Mom and Dad and everyone else, but my heart is in the Mortal Realm. Besides, Marvin wants to go back to his family and I can't leave him."

"I understand," said Aubree. "It'll be strange to not see you every day."

"Hey, you're going to be the next High Queen. You'll be able to come see me whenever you want."

"I haven't decided whether or not I am going to accept," said Aubree.

Marcia put a hand on Aubree's shoulder. "Come on. We both know you are. You can't pass up a chance like that."

"Marcia," called Charity. "It's time to go."

"See you later." Marcia hugged Aubree. "Keep in touch, okay? I don't care how, just do it. Send a letter with Mom and Dad when they visit, maybe. I want to hear every detail of your life."

"Will do," promised Aubree, smiling. "You got the keys to the café from Teegan, right? That place means a lot to me. You take care of it."

"Hey, you know me."

"Yes, I do know you. That's why I'm worried."

Marcia playfully stuck out her tongue. She stepped toward the gate that would send her back to the Mortal Realm. "Love you, cousin!" she called and disappeared.

"I love you, too, cousin," Aubree quietly said to the empty space.

Aubree sat in her room that evening after dinner, thinking about her future. If she turned down the High Queen's offer, then she would still be a Princess. She would never be queen, that was Eirian's job. She would still have her powers, but she would never really understand them or know how to properly use them.

If she accepted, she would learn about her powers and discover how much she could do. She would become High Queen, in time, and have more authority than Eirian ever would, though she knew her sister would never resent her for it. She would get to be with her family either way and Reima would always be by her side.

"What should I do?" she asked Winston. The dog sat in the floor, gnawing on a giant bone. "Should I accept or not?"

Winston looked up at his mistress, head cocked to one side. He barked happily and bounded over to her. He jumped onto her lap and kissed the side of her face.

Aubree laughed. "Are you saying I should go for it?"

Winston barked again and wagged his tail. A knock sounded at the door. Winston jumped off of Aubree's lap and ran, barking, to the door.

"Come in!" called Aubree.

Reima opened the door and leaned down to scratch Winston behind the ears.

"Are you alright?" he asked.

"I'm just trying to decide what to do about the High Queen's offer," said Aubree. "What do you think I should do? And before you say that you can't tell me what to do, remember that this affects you, too."

"I know it does. That is why I am going to be honest with you right now." Reima stood in front of her and took her hands in his. "This is a scary decision and I won't deny that I'm scared too, but I also know that you can handle it."

"But I'll be in charge of the whole Realm," said Aubree. "That's a lot of responsibility."

"That's why you go for the training, first," said Reima. "The High Queen said that training will take years. If you think like a mortal, then that doesn't seem like a long enough time, but you need to remember that you are immortal. When she said 'years' she really meant 'centuries.' She won't make you take over until you are ready."

Aubree smiled and hugged him. "Thank you. I am ready to make my decision now, but I'm glad you're going to be with me."

"I will always be with you," promised Reima.

"I love you, Reima," said Aubree.

"And I love you, Aubree," said Reima.

He pulled her close again, and kissed her.

"I have wanted you to do that since my birthday," smiled Aubree.

"Me too," said Reima.

He smiled back and pulled her in for another, longer, kiss.

Epilogue

Aubree immediately began her studies as future High Queen. Reima began lessons as well, he would be High King at her side. He proposed to Aubree a short time later, however, they did not wed until two years later, when Aubree finally decided she was old enough.

Teegan took the skills she had learned as chef of her café, and used them in the palace kitchen, making the wedding cakes for both Princesses. She remained a close friend to Eirian and was named Godmother to the infant princess, Adelina.

Aubree and Reima had a total of five children, thanks to Reima's wolf blood. The children, also, had lessons under "Grandmother Reya," as the High Queen was affectionately known.

When the time came for Aubree and Reima to be named High Queen and High King, there was a celebration throughout the entire Faerie Realm, the likes of which had not been seen since the coronation of High Queen Reya in time out of memory. Reya stayed just long enough to see that the realm was in good hands before fading away to join her husband.

Marcia and Marvin visited often and eventually returned to stay for good.

The Reign of Aubree and Reima was a long and glorious one. It lasted for many thousands of years and under it, the realm of the Fae flourished.

If you, like Aubree and Eirian, feel like you have your own Tola after you, do not give up hope. Do not let your circumstances tell you who you are. Discover your true identity, and embrace it. You never know what is just around the corner, though the hall seems endless.

Find more Exciting Titles from

JUMPMASTER PRESS™

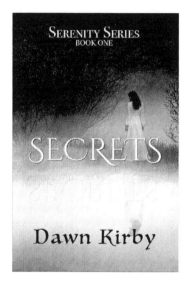

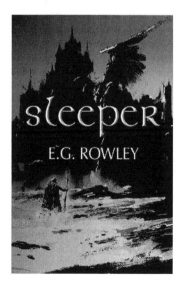

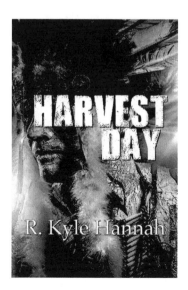

Hidden Identity

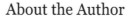

About the Author

Angel LaPoint was born and raised in Alabama and spent many happy holidays in Louisiana with her Cajun father's relatives, so she knows what it is like to live in two different worlds. She currently lives in Alabama with her two cats while she patiently waits for God to bring her Prince Charming into her life.

She has been creating worlds and characters her entire life. She studied fairy tale literature and history in high school, and took creative writing and playwriting courses in college. She enjoys many other creative interests, such as crochet and cosplay. She and her best friend are currently crafting the foundation for a tabletop adventure RPG set in their shared fantasy realm.

Though *Hidden Identity* is her first published work, many more stories are certain to follow.

Hidden Identity